Too Many Deaths

Rosemary Chapple

First published by Busybird Publishing 2025

ISBN:
Print: 978-1-923501-09-6
Ebook: 978-1-923501-10-2

Cover Image: Pixabay

Cover design: Busybird Publishing

Layout and typesetting: Busybird Publishing

Busybird Publishing
2/118 Para Road
Montmorency, Victoria
Australia 3094
www.busybird.com.au

Contents

Prologue

'Come and sit down.' Ivy patted the seat next to her on the leather couch. Geranium remained motionless, staring out of the window.

'I like watching the waves.' Despite Geranium's hesitation, a slight sound of a clearing throat from Ivy encouraged Geranium to take the indicated seat.

'We need to talk.' Normally Ivy would have made Geranium a cup of tea, but she needed the full attention of her friend. 'I think we should move.'

Geranium started a little. 'Move house? Why? I like the sea.'

Ivy acknowledged this with a nod. The house they shared faced directly towards the ocean, and there was an ever-changing vista depending on the weather and the seasons. Ivy paused, then went on 'Darling, the tourists are just appalling now. You can't even get a car park at the supermarket. And the rubbish they leave! Since I moved in with you – it must be two years ago now, I have noticed an increase in traffic. What about a tree change? With the money from selling this house, we could buy a beautiful cottage in a country town, not too far from a hospital, but with everything we need. What do you think?'

'I'm not sure. I've lived here for ten years.' Geranium gazed sadly at the photo of Henry, which sat on the mantlepiece. He was dressed in his lawn bowls gear, the cream colour of the shirt nicely offset by a thick head of grey hair. Geranium remembered when it was taken, not that she ever played lawn bowls – horribly boring game – but Henry had loved it. The club had arranged portraits of all the committee members and presented them at the end of the season. Henry had been very proud of his.

Ivy, having glanced at the photo, looked back at Geranium. 'Yes, but it's not the same without Henry. And we have to find a new cleaner for the house after little Serena was run over and left for dead.'

Geranium nodded slowly, her permed, grey curls bouncing a little. 'I suppose you're right. You usually are. I don't imagine the police will ever find the hit-run driver now.' She paused and sighed. 'We should sell before the house gets too dusty. Where should we go?'

Ivy produced an atlas. 'What about we open it at random and stab a pin in a spot?'

Geranium sparked up. 'That sounds like a good idea.'

They discussed whether to stay in Victoria and, that being decided, Ivy found the double page of maps and pressed a pin into Geranium's hand. 'You do it, darling.' Geranium pursed her lips, shut her eyes and allowed her hand to hover over the page before she carefully placed the pin into the paper.

'There!' She opened her eyes and put on her glasses to read the small print.

'Cow … Cowag … Cowagulac. Never heard of it.'

'But look! There's a big city close by, Balsham. I think it sounds perfect. Decision made?' Geranium looked at Ivy and a tear ran down her cheeks.

'You really think it's a good idea?'

Ivy nodded. 'The best.'

Chapter 1

The main street of Cowagulac was testimony to the difficulties that country towns were experiencing. Several of the shops were empty and boarded up. One of the farm supply businesses had given up the battle, though a rival expanded on the main street. The op shop, however, was thriving thanks to an effective system which exchanged goods donated in Cowagulac with those in Balsham and surrounds.

Most of the houses were standard weatherboard, somewhat faded, and, in many cases, with paint peeling off the most exposed side. It was difficult to keep an interesting and attractive garden thanks to the erratic nature of the rainfall, but it's location in a valley gave Cowagulac the advantage of milder winters and a higher rainfall than surrounding areas. The plant most likely to succeed was the agapanthus, which bloomed excessively in purple and white in most gardens.

An initial inspection of the available housing had given Geranium and Ivy a few choices. The estate agent tried to convince them of a property further out of town, but they knew the moment they laid eyes on *Mermaid Views* that this would suit them perfectly. Although one house, it was set out like two units with a common lounge area. To the right of the large dining area was a bedroom and bathroom, which was mirrored to the left. A neat kitchen and laundry were directly ahead.

'Perfect. We will have our own space as well as the chance to watch TV together in the evenings!' Ivy was enchanted. 'And look at the kitchen at the back. It's facing Mermaid Mountain.'

Geranium prowled around the kitchen, pulling open drawers and sliding windows, letting in a blast of hot air that hit Ivy in the face. Gently, Ivy shut the windows and led Geranium to the kitchen. She tended to treat Geranium as the child she never had, and this had become more intense since Henry had died. Geranium found it easier to acquiesce.

'We can watch the sunset every night while we wash the dishes, or walk in the morning as the sun is rising.'

'When have you ever been up with the sunrise?' Geranium snorted.

'And when did you last wash the dishes?' In the past, banter between the pair had been commented on by concerned onlookers who thought they were serious, but they understood each other well enough to finish each other's sentences.

Their offer was accepted on the spot. The house by the beach had sold for a good price, so there was plenty of money for renovations if necessary. In a couple of months, the moving truck had delivered their furniture, and the two elderly friends were settled and comfortable.

***

'Hurry up, Geranium, we don't want to miss anything. I've never been to a cockroach race before.' Ivy leaned across, opened the passenger door and drummed her fingers on the steering wheel as Geranium emerged, swinging her carry bag over her shoulder and wandering unhurriedly through the front gate.

While Geranium fumbled with her seat belt, Ivy headed for the short stretch of bitumen that ran down Cucuracha Road.

'What road do I take to get to Maniagallup?' Ivy didn't have a good sense of direction, and Ivy driving in the city traffic had some terrifying moments. It wasn't so bad out here in the country, with quiet roads, though the occasional slow-moving tractor caused a little frustration.

'Left at the next turn.' Geranium consulted a road map, with big print suitable for deteriorating eyesight. They both had mobile phones, but using technology for maps was beyond them.

'I can't wait to get started on our workshops,' Geranium said, as they navigated the roundabout. 'I think it was the most exciting thing I read in the local paper – that they run a whole variety of training sessions, and that people were welcome to apply to present courses. How lucky that we arrived in the village at just the right time? With our skills, the homemade memory class is bound to be a success, and it'll help us get accepted too.'

'I'm sure it will mean a great deal to these people to get their stories told. It's refreshing – no one would have been interested in a class like this in the city. What do you think of the name *Ivy's Homemade Memories*? Unless you want to call it Ivy *and* Geranium's Homemade Memories.' Ivy didn't want to insult Geranium by leaving her off the title, but Ivy knew that most of the work would fall to her. Geranium was good at starting things but not so good at finishing them.

'Don't worry about me. It's a perfect name. They're such a creative town, I mean, the community centre is such an inventive way to convert a cow shed.'

'So many interests, too,' Ivy rejoined. 'Art, writing, singing, and those interesting chainsaw sculptures of Ned's – he doesn't do just cows and sheep – he does people and buildings too. But it's a sheep shed – don't say cow shed or you'll offend the locals.' Ivy swerved to avoid a possum which came scampering across the road chasing a late morning snack.

'Well, whatever, I don't regret our tree change. Such a quiet little place, so much creativity, amid all the peace and beauty of the ranges. And it's just perfect to have our little cotta— Stop!' Geranium screeched. 'Pull over.'

Ivy slammed her foot on the brake, skidding on the gravel as she slid to a stop behind a bushy roadside wattle and stared at a lone figure wandering along near the shops up ahead. 'Whoever could that be? Everyone is at the races. Wait, it's that wretched politician who's been demanding the workshops on workshopping. I don't need to talk to him. Is he looking for a lift?'

'Don't move, he hasn't seen us. I'd never let him in my car.'

They watched the man glance back along Cucuracha Road, looking at the town's small offering of stores. He seemed to have come from that direction, and they wondered what he'd been doing. *Likely casing local businesses hoping to find some people to listen to his speech,* Ivy thought. Clearly, he wasn't a local as he didn't understand why the shops were all closed on this Saturday morning – the importance of the cockroach race could not be understated.

A quick U-turn enabled the two ladies to watch him through the rear-view mirror. News of his plan to make everyone complete training on how to run a workshop had spread like wildfire among the community. No one had the time or energy to sit through a useless course just to satisfy some government idiocy, but there was a threat that they wouldn't be allowed to continue the classes unless they all completed the training, so he was not a popular figure in the village.

Standing in the shade of the deserted milk bar in eerie stillness, waving away a blowfly that was sucking on his sweat beads, the politician lowered his dark glasses. He stared at the grassy circle at the base of the town's flagpole, located not far from the shops and headed over to examine the unusual chain fence around the flagpole.

These were no ordinary posts, but rather reclaimed piles from some collapsed wharf. Each of the four posts was an extraordinary, well, work of art it might be called. The first was vaguely recognisable as a possum – or maybe a wombat – crawling sideways up a tree. He strolled around to inspect a short, scantily clad, one-legged woman with the chain link inserted through her abdomen. He wrinkled his nose at the third post; a cup and saucer, or maybe a mug. It was hard to tell. The fourth was either a trumpet or a lily. He wondered if they were still to be painted.

His curiosity aroused, he knelt on the weedy grass to inspect a plaque that read: *Created by Ned Christophers, chainsaw artist. Cowagulac, 2010, under a grant for emerging artists.* The politician shook his head, amazed this Christophers chap was actually paid for this most extraordinary and, frankly, unpleasant set of sculptures.

Ivy and Geranium watched on as he continued his fruitless search for an audience, eventually heading for the pub which might at least furnish him with a cold pint. He paused to examine a lamppost carved into what one could only assume to be a police officer, followed by one in the shape of a rather unfortunate firefighter, and, finally, a paramedic standing beside an ambulance that was in desperate need of a trip to the mechanic.

Outside the library, a log had been fashioned into a pile of books – more or less.

Passing a bedraggled wooden building that was once the council offices before Balsham grew to become the main centre, he stopped, and the two onlookers saw him do a double take. Under the shade of the large peppercorn tree, where a comfortable bench had been intended for sitting and chatting, stood Ned's pièce de résistance. As if in a fit of vindictiveness, the entire seat had been hacked into jagged saw teeth, each some half metre high. It was only when he walked around the back of the structure that he saw the title: *Surf's up at Cowagulac.* If anyone had been close enough, they would have heard him mutter 'But Cowagulac is 400 kilometres from the beach. What the heck?'

'We're going to be so late,' Ivy whispered as the politician walked back past the closed pub, wiped his patent leather shoes free of a cow pat and climbed into his four-wheel drive. 'Let's get going.' She tugged at Geranium's arm. 'People who don't support the town at the Cockroach Races are not much respected, I'm told, and by now we might have completely missed them. It's the entertainment of the year!'

'I certainly don't want to lose the respect of our new neighbours,' Geranium agreed.

Meanwhile, out at the cockroach races, Maniagallup Valley's bookie had been gathering all the money to be squandered on the competition. Everyone knew that Cowagulac grew the biggest and fiercest cockroaches, and the neighbouring towns didn't stand a chance. Nevertheless, betting was eager, especially on Maniagallup's *Prince of Peace*, a glistening, beady-eyed roach. The Valley folk were sure that this year Prince would well and truly defeat *Cowcocky Blues*, champion of the previous two years.

Parking the car in the one remaining space, fortunately in the shade of a large gum tree, Ivy and Geranium joined the moving line of people surrounding the course to take their turn at watching a race.

Prince of Peace and *Cowcocky Blues* were meeting in the last race of the calendar, by which time the running pitch was bare and dusty. The audience had migrated to the best viewing spots. The official announcer, Lancelot, was by this time nearly hoarse, having commentated on all races on the card. Despite this, his voice came through the loudhailer powerfully, his slight stutter booming through the crowd.

'Now for the f-final race on this m-memorable day. L-last bets should be placed immediately with Charlie. Stand back, the contestants are be-being brought out. F-firstly we have

Prince of Peace. This f-fine roach is out of *WaranPeace*, sired by *Ulysses*. A warm welcome to the Prince.' Maniagallup supporters cheered and clapped. 'And now f-for the champion, *Cowcocky Blues*. Sired by *Dusty Winter*, out of *S-sunset Pink*. For the past two years, Cowcocky has been unbeatable. Ladies and gentlemen, these two fine roaches are ready to run. S-stand clear. They're off!'

A low buzz grew in volume and intensity as the roaches set off down the straight.

'Cowcocky's wandering off the track … now he's coming back. Maybe that was his plan all along. The Prince is edging out Cowcocky with a f-flick of his hind leg. Not sure that's allowed.'

Lancelot continued as the cheers and heckling grew.

'Cowcocky's coming home with a rush, as expected, it's Cowcocky, Cowcocky by a f-feeler, it's game, s-set and match to Cowcocky again, third year in a r-r-r-row!'

The crowd cheered, then slowly started to dissipate. Geranium and Ivy edged their way out. A lumpish, pasty woman suddenly appeared in front of Ivy and Geranium, flinging out her hands and crying, 'Oh, you're the new girls!' and gave them each a welcoming hug. 'I'm Laura, remember? I'll be organising the workshop timetable, and you're running one, aren't you? Or both of you?'

'Ivy's running the Family History and Memoir one. I haven't quite decided yet.'

'You're Ivy, and you're Geranium. Have I got that right?'

They nodded. 'I'm the taller one,' Geranium commented. Ivy lowered her brows.

'You're taller by *two centimetres*. On a good day.' Geranium gave her a not-so-friendly shove to the elbow.

Laura reddened and rushed to change the subject. 'Wasn't that a great race? Did you win?'

Ivy shook her head. 'No time to bet. We're mainly here hoping to get to know people.'

'I saw you arrive; you nearly missed the last race,' she paused. 'Did you get lost?'

'Oh, no,' Geranium hastened to assure her. 'We were just …'

She glanced at Ivy, who chimed in with, 'We had to avoid that unpleasant politician who wants to make everyone take workshops on workshopping.'

'That stupid man. He should have been here, but he mustn't have even checked his dates. And he thinks he can tell us what to do and how to do it. At least you made it in time for me to take you round and introduce you.' She took Geranium's arm and pulled her, stumbling, in the direction of the sound system, but Lancelot had already vanished.

As Ivy caught up, Laura opened her bag and presented Ivy with a packet of chocolates. 'Here you are. Do take some, Ivy.' Ivy shook her head while Geranium waved a negating hand, but they both found themselves with a handful each.

Some of the chocolates spilt to the ground unnoticed as Laura steered Geranium towards a rangy man in overalls with a tattooed arm that was waving a chainsaw. With a short beard and his hair tied back, the five gold rings in his left ear were visible. 'Ned!' Laura called, beckoning him towards them, a chainsaw advancing towards her face. 'Come and meet Ivy and Geranium. Poor things, they were late because that wretched politician was lurking in town.'

'What the hell's he hanging round for? Hasn't he done enough?' The mere mention was enough to provoke Ned's ire. The politician wanted to allow logging in Ned's beloved and protected forest, where the biggest trees occasionally provided him with gigantic logs for sculpting, and witchetty grubs to secretly augment his diet. 'They want to fence off my forest. What stupidity is that? Next thing they'll start logging it and then where will we be?' He ranted to Laura for some time, ignoring the newcomers who stood shrinking from the waving chainsaw, silently impressed. Eventually, he extended a rough hand to give each of them a bouncing shake before turning his back and stalking off. Laura gazed after him.

Picnicking groups were collapsing onto rugs all over the paddock as Laura apologised for Ned's rudeness. 'It's the food that does it, you know, he's a vegetarian, and I'm sure he doesn't get enough carbs.' She grasped at her stomach. 'I'm getting an upset stomach myself, just thinking about how angry he got at that man's proposal. Poor Ned!' She gulped down a couple of chocolates from her packet. 'This always soothes it,' she added. 'I so wish he would let me help him.' She turned to watch him with a faraway look in her eyes. Geranium and Ivy exchanged glances. It was obvious that Laura had a 'thing' for the ear-ringed Ned and equally obvious that the older ladies could not fathom the attraction.

Following the races, entertainment had been organised. Laura excused herself to round up the performers, rearranging them several times before gripping the microphone and breathily announcing, 'Introducing my own sister Karen Adams, winner of last year's prize for most alike owner and dog. She will demonstrate her incredible training abilities with her Irish Wolfhound, Whisky Darling.'

Ivy gasped at the size of the hairy dog. His front paws hugged Karen's shoulders as he stood on his hind legs. Ivy was soon amazed at his skill and obedience as he sat a toddler in her chair, brought her a plate of sandwiches and tucked her potty under the chair. Laura clapped adoringly as the animal leapt down into the crowd, screaming when Ned failed to scatter with the rest of the crowd and narrowly avoided amputating Whisky Darling's adorable nose with the chainsaw.

'Oh! Ned! Are you all right? You should've moved. I mean … Laura looked him over anxiously as Whisky Darling thrust a ball into the hands of another small child and dragged him by the T-shirt, dumping him beside the other toddler.

Ivy was gasping. 'Ned should be more careful. I hate to see anybody with something as dangerous as a chainsaw near little children.'

'Clever he may be, but he shouldn't be allowed out in public with that thing! I think I'd fence him in that forest reserve he was carrying on about and not let him out,' Geranium added.

'On his own? But what if he had an accident?' Ivy asked.

'Don't you think I've done enough training in workplace health and safety? If a child got their head mown off, the Cowagulac community would be up for damages that would bankrupt them. It's always the way when someone dies unexpectedly.'

Laura was calming the crowd with a breathy recitation of one of her own hard-to-hear poems. 'Isn't that one of the ones Laura sent us to read? It was bad then, and I don't think she has adopted any of our excellent suggestions.'

Next, Laura introduced Dora Beattie, who was wearing a slinky, sequinned gown which was more suited for someone ten years younger than her. She gave an off-key rendering of the top-of-the-pops melody, 'LGB, TQI, our love reaches to the sky,' which caused Geranium to wince and cover her ears.

Eventually, when the items were over and the Cucuracha Road Catharist Church Choir began to sing their anthem, 'A Curse on the Cockroach', people started to pack up their beer cans and Tupperware containers of Iced VoVos to head back home. Laura's desperate voice followed them over the loudspeaker: 'And I nearly forgot to remind all you workshoppers that the planning meeting is Wednesday night, don't forget!'

Chapter 2

Balsham had overtaken Cowagulac as the main hub of the region some twenty years ago. Cowagulac residents held a bitter grudge towards Balsham, which, in the view of the locals was a far inferior town. The area was principally known for wheat farming with some sheep and other useful crops of various sorts of peas. There had been a battle between the two towns over the site of the community centre, but Cowagulac, with a magnificent barn venue available, had won the day, and with the help of a grant, the town was able to make a most attractive community centre which other villages could use, should they dare to.

The workshop planning meeting was to be held at the Cowagulac Community Cultural Centre (CCCC) headquarters. The venue might more properly have been called a Shedquarters, for it was, in fact, an old shearing shed. Before the building was converted, it had greasy floorboards and a slightly rusty corrugated iron roof, in traditional Australian style. The latter was fixed courtesy of The Leaky Tap, a plumbing business just out of Cowagulac. In sponsoring the repairs, they had creatively left their advertising slogan painted onto the roof as a permanent reminder to those flying over it. Still, the building maintained that rustic look which was so appealing.

The stained shearing stalls had been removed, and the wooden floor reconditioned. The old sorting table remained, functioning as a committee table, which was sometimes inconvenient because it dominated one half of the large meeting room. The new kitchenette had the essentials, including a large pie warmer for the footy club awards nights. With the addition of heating and air con, it was a valuable building for the town, even though newcomers sometimes turned up their nose with a sniff, imagining they smelt sweat and sheep droppings and could hear the shouts of 'tar here' from brawny, bare-chested shearers. Geranium commented to Ivy that she would have quite liked to see some brawny, bare-chested shearers. The whole set up was complemented by a gravel car park and some new garden beds which were still bare.

With only a few minutes till the meeting was scheduled to start, Geranium, much to Ivy's annoyance, dashed back inside to make sure the back door was locked, even though country folk usually left their doors either unlocked or wide open altogether for cooling. Neighbours might, after all, need to borrow a cup of sugar.

Ivy impatiently drummed her fingers on the steering wheel, until Geranium ran back to the car, thrusting the house keys into her handbag. Accelerating speedily, Ivy left skid marks in the gravel.

'Oh, stop for a moment, Ivy!' They had reached the top of the hill, and Ivy, sighing heavily, stopped. Geranium got out and stood gazing at the mountain range.

'I love this view,' Geranium sighed. 'It really does look like a reclining mermaid, doesn't it?' Ivy, who had a less vivid imagination than Geranium, agreed in order to hurry her friend back into the car.

Finally, they turned into the driveway of the Cowagulac Community Cultural Centre and parked outside the door of the adjoining café.

'Look Ivy, I don't see why you had to pester me about running late. Laura's here but we're the only other car. We'll have plenty of time for a coffee. Laura said Rosie will give us one even if she's officially closed. She doesn't mind staying on duty, says she prefers it to leaving the café to volunteers.'

Laura turned from the counter to greet them, coffee in hand. Ivy raised her eyebrows at the voluminous orange top Laura was wearing over her purple slacks, but smiled and nodded, hoping Laura's organisational skills were stronger than her clothing selection abilities. Smoothing her own neat blouse over rounded hips, Ivy silently congratulated herself on her dignified, grey outfit, lifted by a discreet, colourful scarf. Silk, of course.

Laura approached with outstretched arms, sloshing liquid onto the floor. With an exasperated gasp Rosie ran around from behind the counter with a cloth and knelt before them.

'Oh dear! Oh, Auntie Rosie I'm so sorry. How careless of me, I'll put it down.' Laura shrank back out of the way and reached her wet, cup-laden hand towards a table.

'Not there. You know that table's reserved for the oldies and the feeble, and you're neither.'

'Oh, I know, I know, I'm so sorry. I wasn't going to sit there, believe me, Auntie Rosie. I wouldn't do that, you know

I wouldn't.' Sheepishly, Laura gestured towards another table and Ivy pulled out chairs for herself and Geranium. Eventually, Laura was settled, and Rosie hovered around them.

'I suppose you want coffee too,' Auntie Rosie said to Ivy and Geranium. 'How do you like it?'

'Extra hot latte for me and a short black for Ivy, please.'

'I loved your poems,' Geranium beamed at Laura. 'It was kind of you to send them to us. I've mainly written memoirs and short stories, but I'd love to be able to write like that. I start a lot of poems, but, in my view, poems have to rhyme and follow a rhythm, you know, dumpty, dumpty, dumpty dum, and then I get stuck. When is your workshop?'

'No, no, I'm not running a workshop, just the organising. I do regular tea leaf readings in the café, because people like them, and I feel I'm giving pleasure to somebody. I couldn't pretend to teach anybody how to write poetry. When I write, it just seems to flow.'

The sound of a heavy vehicle pulling into the car park with a grinding of the gears echoed through the shed. Moments later, the door was pushed open and a man walked in.

'Oh, hello, Klaus,' Laura piped up. 'Have you met Ivy and Geranium? They're helping to write local biographies. I didn't see you at the cockroach races.'

'Ah, I'm to those sorts of things not going. I'm Klaus Fuchs. Numerology, astral travelling and UFOs.' With a modicum of his face visible amid flowing, white hair and whiskers, he extended a hand to them in turn. 'You will to my workshop come?' Klaus's speech was often arranged with the verb at the end of the sentence. It took a bit of getting used to but added charm to his often long-winded stories.

'Well, no. We are running our own workshops,' Ivy told him. 'I'm afraid numerology is not my area of expertise.'

Geranium shook her head. 'I've travelled all over the world, but I'm afraid astral travelling isn't among my interests.'

'Ah, you don't understand … I haven't actually done any astral travelling yet, but my experience with UFOs in this area something fascinating is.'

Rosie butted in, 'You must hear about all Klaus's experiences! I've had sightings too and I can assure you …' It suddenly seemed that everybody was arriving at once, and the conversation was lost amid a hubbub of greetings. The locals moved to the chairs set out around the large shearing table. Geranium, who had a vivid imagination, could almost hear the shearers' calls and see the heavy fleeces being tossed onto the table for sorting and rolling.

Bony Karen Adams acknowledged her plump sister, Laura, with a wave of the hand before turning to place a rolled-up piece of painted paper on another table. Behind her, a woman Geranium recognised as Jill appeared at the glass door only to be pushed aside by a huge, furry form whose nose and paws rested on the glass, higher than her head. 'Oh no, darling!' Karen turned to make decisive hand movements, and the animal sat. 'Back in the car!' The dog disappeared. 'It's all right, Jill. He just wants to be friends with everybody.'

Hands pushing against the weighty door, Jill sidled in, head turned to keep a wary eye open for the dog. 'He's back in the van. But shouldn't he be tied up?'

'I couldn't do that to my beautiful Dumpling. It's so unfair that he's not allowed in here. Colleen can't leave the new puppies so he's lonely, poor thing. He's *such* a good boy, my Dumpling, and he always does exactly what he's told. Erm, almost always. Just look at my latest painting – isn't he just darling?' She picked up the paper from the table, unrolled it, and held it up as she beamed around the room. It was an extraordinary piece of work. Dumpling seemed to be three-dimensional, standing out from the background of light pastels, but no one took any notice except for Ivy, who nodded and smiled politely.

Jill, turning to look, forced a smile, muttering that, however nice the dog, he would not be the subject of her planned wall murals. She squeezed a chair in next to Ivy. 'Your workshop is going to be on writing, isn't it? I'm planning artworks to decorate the town. We need something more than chainsaw posts and the Mermaid Range to attract the tourists. I thought we could do a series like the painted water tanks. You know the ones; lots of people go from town to town to look at them. Our town could become famous for the murals.'

Geranium still had her thoughts on the mountain range. 'When you look at them together, those summits along the skyline really do look like a Mermaid, don't they Jill? You can see the lot, the head, boobs, tummy, even those peaks that look like the tail standing up. Have you painted it?'

'Not yet. I usually do theatrical set design and scenery painting, but my workshop is probably going to be in creative costume, and I think my ideas …'

Her words were drowned by Auntie Rosie's voice rising as she told Ivy, 'Of course dogs are not allowed in. Let me tell you what happened when Klaus brought his mutt in to save it from being eaten by aliens, and he …'

Dora Beattie followed her agent, Ingrid, through the door, quietly singing the words to the song she was planning to record – 'I cannot believe, no I cannot believe, in an interventionist deity, but,' with Ingrid persistently speaking over her, discussing her plans for the launch of Dora's single at the CCCC.

Thankful at last to be making some use of her qualifications in Fine Arts and Public Relations, if only to employ her virtuosity in language, Ingrid was proud of her passionate editing of the lyrics to avoid cliché and had taken Dora under her wing with the intent of improving her vocabulary. The song was, by any standard, eccentric, but Ingrid felt that it could find a niche in the market somewhere. However, despite her involvement in Dora's career, Ingrid's planned workshop was to be on applying for grants. She had applied for several grants to enable Dora to record an album, which would begin her career. Ingrid hailed Lancelot Charger and Ned Christophers as they burst in behind her, summoning them to take a seat at the table and explain sound systems to her.

Lancelot's hair transplant and neat military moustache may have been a contrast to the exuberance of Klaus's white mane and trailing whiskers. He avoided accompanying rangy Ned when possible, despising the gold-ringed augmentation of his appearance, but no amount of strutting could disguise the insignificance of Lancelot's stature as Ned towered over him.

'Good evening, all,' Lancelot greeted them, his ringing radio voice, currently without its usual stammer. He inspected the assembled group with assurance, believing with certainty that he could plan and organise the new term for the CCCC with more effect than Laura.

Ned strode to inspect the foodstuffs offering in the café's glass counter. Frowning, he bent over it, barking 'Cappuccino, almond milk,' at Auntie Rosie before grimacing at the selection and turning his back on it, the end of his long lank hank of dark hair flopping on the glass. 'Can't you stock some real food?' He nodded in the direction of some remaining pies and sausage rolls, his horse-like ponytail whipping along the counter. 'Who eats that disgusting stuff?'

'Everybody else,' retorted Rosie, glancing with distaste at the gold rings in his left ear lobe. 'And get that hair off my counter. Nobody wants dandruff flavoured coffee.' Ned might be fanatical about natural foods and natural bush, but she thought there was nothing natural about those ornaments, hair allowed to hang below his waist, or arms and chest tattooed with birds and flowers.

'When you're r-ready, Ned.' Lancelot's raised voice reached all ears and conversation began to dwindle. 'I'll just check my lis-st before we b-begin. Money-raising proposals f-first: Jill Taylor, canine art exhibition to raise money for town murals. Laura Adams, poetry readings, and Karen Adams, portraiture exhibition. Dora Beattie, CD launch. And Ned's always getting on with those chainsaw sculptures without waiting for a grant.' Ned stifled his desire to say a few words with a glare as Lancelot continued.

'Auntie Rosie continues to look after our venue.' She raised a hesitant hand, and he nodded at her.

'I want to ask you about that time when we ran out of coffee and I ...' Rosie began.

Lancelot shook his head and continued, speaking over her, 'Laura Adams, financial adviser and—' He turned his head to stare doubtfully at Laura Adams. 'F-financial adviser and money raising coordinator.' Auntie Rosie had continued her coffee request *sotto voce* and was concluding, '… so what do you want me to do about it?'

'Later, Rosie! Now the workshops. Klaus Fuchs, numerology and astral travelling?'

Ned's face contorted into a sneer. Klaus rose from his seat and opened his mouth. 'Sit down, Klaus!' Lancelot continued without giving anyone the chance to comment. 'Ned Christophers. Conservation?' His eyebrows rose as astonishment dropped his chin. Incredulously he repeated, 'Ned Christophers's workshop is on conservation?'

'Real conservation,' Ned roared, rising. 'Not that mad Greenie stuff!'

Klaus yelled back, 'And your qualifications? What makes you such an expert on conservation? You and that locked shed of yours with humming machinery, that doesn't sound too conservative for me. Where are your solar panels? And your water tanks?'

The meeting had become chaotic as people tried to have their say about whatever pet subject was on their mind.

Ned's voice rose over the hubbub. 'Hogwash. It's experience that counts, not bits of paper!'

Auntie Rosie rushed to his rescue. 'You know how sick he was after he ate that …'

'Later!' Lancelot bellowed. 'Sit down everyone. We haven't finished.' It took some time before the meeting came back to order. Lancelot continued, 'Now, Ingrid, applying for grants. Hasn't everybody already applied for grants?'

Ingrid stood. 'I have qualifications, as you well know, in fine arts and public relations and I believe this can satisfy the ludicrous new requirement for a totally redundant workshoppers' workshop.'

'That is for f-further discussion. We all know the ridiculous government demands for course.'

The sound of the sliding door opening caused everyone to turn their heads. A polished black shoe stepped over the threshold, followed by a grey, suit-clad leg, and, finally, the body and head of the local politician. A collective sigh combined with a groan emanated from the members of the committee. Ned thrust back his chair.

'What the hell are you doing here? No one invited you.'

James Thurber, MP, tiptoed into the room, as though that would make him less conspicuous.

'Well, I thought I would see how you are coming along. We're aware the government directive has caused some in the community to be concerned, and I wanted to reassure you that we are fully supportive of the local community's interests, and are always open to community consultation. Let me be very clear, we are one hundred and twenty percent focused on meeting community expectations.'

Ned's jaw dropped. 'Don't you need basic maths to be a politician? There's no hundred and twenty percent!'

James Thurber, MP waved a hand as though to indicate the malleability of mathematics when it came to politics. 'I want to assure all of you that we aim to deliver key outcomes to all of our stakeholders with a locked-in budget specifically targeted to best outcomes on this project.'

Lancelot had by now pulled Ned's sleeve to stop him advancing further. Ned shook it off with a toss of his long locks.

'Jibber jabber jibber jabber, that's all you blokes ever do.' He stalked to the kitchen and ran himself a glass of water.

The rest of the group had remained silent, but all stared at James Thurber, MP. Lancelot took up the cudgels. 'I'm sure we all appreciate you coming, but this is a committee meeting, and we would like to continue with our agenda. Maybe you could make an appointment next time.'

A weak smile hovered on the lips of James Thurber (MP). 'As your MP, let's see if we can all get on the same page here. I've been very clear that we are engaging with locals in a variety of ways, to ensure that our outcome-driven implementation of policy is aimed at delivering what is needed in the community. We have always been fully transparent and committed to achieving this, and I have complete faith in our staff delivering exactly that.'

Ingrid pushed her chair back energetically. 'Perhaps you would care to run a course in plain speaking, because personally, I find it an affront that you come here, spouting words like 'supportive' and 'consultation' when you don't mean it. Perhaps you could take the information-scrambling black hole out of your nether regions and actually speak without obfuscation and a relentless devotion to 'outcome-driven' hokum. This coterie does not need your advisement, however bodacious you may believe it to be. My strong recommendation is that you absquatulate.'

'Well! That's a warm country welcome. Remind me of it when your grant application is submitted.'

James Thurber, MP, backed away, muttering apologies and exited abruptly. A hubbub broke out immediately.

'What cheek!'

'How dare he?'

'Who does he think he is anyway?'

'Community consultation my arse,' Klaus chimed in at the last moment.

'Now, quiet please. We have seen him on his way, so let's get on.'

Slowly, order was resumed and Lancelot carried on as though nothing had happened. 'Lastly comes my own course: Lancelot Ch-charger, how to present a radio program. However, we have newcomers in our midst. Ivy Vine and Geranium Golightly, who might wish to present a course themselves. What are you offering?'

Ivy stood, holding her head high. 'I would like to introduce my friend, Geranium Golightly,' she glanced down, 'who will support me in running some sessions on family history and memoir writing. That is, after we have all completed the required course. My years as a legal secretary have taught me there's no escaping the demands of legislation.' Geranium looked around with a nod and a pleasant smile.

There was a moment of silence, before Lancelot verbalised what most of the group were probably thinking.

'With due respect, we don't feel we need this course to do what we have been doing for several years.' Murmurs grew louder as people started to respond to Ivy's implied criticism.

Ned sneered. 'Rubbish! My qualifications are in life experience, and no stupid course is going to improve my presentations.' He stood, hands on hips.

'S-s-silence!' Lancelot thrust his chair back, glaring. 'Ned Christophers. If you require a workshop on manners, I'm sure Laura can organise one.'

'Don't talk to me about manners,' Ned hissed. 'Or numbers. What sort of neighbour breeds thousands of bees that sting me, smokes me out with bonfires, stinks me out with his vile seaweed mulch ...?'

Klaus chimed in. 'Ha! And the constant noise of your chainsaws going night and day makes me sleep good never.'

'Enough! Both of you. Now, let's have a break for a drink before we resume.'

He turned to Auntie Rosie, 'More coffee all round.' As she bustled off, he stalked to the door and stood breathing in the fresh night air, slowly, rhythmically. After Rosie had served everybody else, she came over to Lancelot with a mug of hot chocolate and a marshmallow. He thanked and complimented her, slowly and elegantly, with a not-too-patronising smile.

'Oh, Lancelot, I don't think it's such a bad idea to have these workshoppers' workshops, not for everybody, of course, I don't mean that, I think that's wrong. But just to help one or two who might ...'

'Talk it over with the others, Aunt Rose.' He turned to face outdoors and resumed deep breathing, punctuated with sips of hot chocolate, before tapping his pencil on the cup. Meanwhile, people slowly returned to their seats.

'Ahem! If that's all the cultural proposals ...'

Ivy raised her hand tentatively. 'I'm not sure if our memoir writing workshop comes under *cultural* or *history*.' She smiled at Lancelot and leaned in towards him.

'We don't yet have a history section, so I'll include it under cultural. Now, we need to address the government directive about the cultural and administrative training session. I'm sure none of us feel we need this, but if the CCCC is to retain any current, or apply for any further, government grants, every instructor must attend this three-hour course. I propose that we engage a trainer and arrange a time when we can all come. I can't issue the booklet offering this season's courses until this is complete. Comments, anyone?' He looked around enquiringly. There was a mumble of comments from individuals, all in a tone of voice which suggested the government decree was unwelcome, and that there was a place where they could shove their training course.

Ingrid raised her hand. 'I am prepared to run the course. Obviously, it will take a bit of work to prepare, but I'm qualified to do it.'

Lancelot looked at her and pursed his lips before replying, 'Very well, thank you. I'll email you the government directive.'

Once more he tapped his pencil. 'We can moan and complain all we like – and I like more than anyone – but the fact remains, we have to do it. Does Saturday the 14th suit everyone? Two o'clock to five o'clock?' Almost instantly, the evening's second chorus of protests followed.

'What about my dog show?'

'I need to rehearse my song.'

'I've got to get on with my chainsaw art.'

'I usually paint on Saturday afternoons when the light is good.'

'Enough,' Lancelot raised his voice. 'Anyone who isn't prepared to come will not be presenting their workshop and might as well leave now.'

Silence fell over the room. Ivy and Geranium looked at each other uneasily. Klaus stroked his beard. Jill pulled at her T-shirt. Ingrid looked at her laptop and tapped the keys imperiously. Laura exhaled with an exasperated sigh, but no one got up to leave.

'Very well then. I'll send the form in tomorrow. Now, let's discuss your workshops in more detail. Since the only new workshop this term is Ivy and Geranium's, I'm going to first ask them to give us some more information.'

Ivy tapped her papers together and nodded to Geranium, who smiled gently at the group before proceeding. Laura was a bit surprised to hear her speak. Ivy always seemed to be the bossier of the two. 'Well, as you know, we are new to the Cowagulac community, but we are very impressed with the range of talent and the warm welcome we have received. Ivy and I are both experienced writers. Ivy has worked in the corporate sector and her report writing has been used as a model for businesses. I have some volumes of the memoirs I have written for other people which I can show you if you'd like. Our idea is to create a workshop where people can talk about their families and the history of the area, and we would help them put these words on paper. We would start with a private session for each participant to set goals and outline their story. At the end of the series, we plan to create a volume of either short biographies or stories with a historical connection to the area. This could be self-funded, in that sales in the community should cover the modest cost.

However, a seeding grant would be useful as a buffer so that we don't need to ask the members to contribute to the publication.'

Silence followed Geranium's monologue. She didn't dare look around to see the expressions on the faces of the group. Then, she heard a slow clapping begin and turned bright red. She looked up to see Lancelot leading what quickly grew to substantial applause. 'That sounds most interesting,' Laura said as the gathering rose to adjourn back to the café. She continued, 'I haven't even started writing but I have such a lot in my head. There are many things I know about the area, and I think some of them have been buried in the past. Maybe they should remain there. But you can advise me on that.'

Ivy looked around in time to catch Klaus stepping away as though he had been eavesdropping. Lancelot approached from the other side.

'My, your sessions look like they will be popular,' he commented. 'I wonder what people will write about. As the radio presenter, I can assure you that emotions sometimes run very high in this town. There are passions that are hidden, as you have seen tonight.'

'Until tonight, Cowagulac has seemed so peaceful,' Ivy reflected. But, yes, you're right, I can certainly see the passion that was hidden under the surface.' Noticing Rosie holding out a cup of tea and a plate of biscuits, Ivy quickly accepted. 'Oh, thank you dear.' Rosie scuttled away, deftly side-stepping Ned who had his hand held out in an effort to stop her.

'What do feelings run so deeply about?' Geranium had been sipping quietly but now joined in the conversation.

'Well, we are a bit insular, you know. Young people today move away, and we don't get as many itinerants in to pick fruit or help with the harvest. Some of them used to stay and become part of the community. Now, the farmers can get by with a few machines and a couple of workers. The community spirit isn't there anymore. But there have been some times when,' he lowered his voice, 'when people think that other people have done things to people that those people didn't deserve and that upsets people.' He nodded slowly and essayed a wink a Geranium and Ivy. And with that cryptic gesture, he moved away.

***

'I didn't have a clue what he was talking about, all that people this and people that,' Ivy said as they were on their way home.

'Did you glean any more gossip? I saw you chatting to Laura. She seems to know what's going on.'

'Laura was telling me about her sister, Karen, and the dogs. Apparently, she's quite fanatical about them. But she's a good trainer, Laura said.'

Ivy chuckled. 'I heard Jill say she's scared stiff of anything larger than a chihuahua. Personally, I find those little things yappy and unpleasant. I'd rather Karen's wolfhounds any day.'

'Well, lucky you. I got caught by Ingrid. I have to say, I didn't understand a word of what she was saying, even though it was English. She has such a vocabulary! I don't think I've ever heard anyone use 'matusalemic' and 'exophthalmic' in a sentence before. In fact, I know I haven't.'

'What on earth? What do they mean? And how could she have used them in a sentence?'

'Matusalemic is something about a collection of sacred Hebrew scriptures, and exophthalmic is where your eye bulges out of the socket. I had to ask her. I can't even remember how she strung them together. Something about when she was writing Dora's song about an interventionist deity, how Methuselah's eye bulged out, or something like that. No good asking me, you need to talk to her.'

'No thanks.' Ivy slammed the car door. 'I'll leave that to you. Good night, I'm excited about our workshop.'

'Me, too.' The two women reached their front door. Geranium paused as she pushed her key in the lock. 'I'm still keen to do that workshop on common garden poisons and their antidotes. But maybe Cowagulac isn't ready for that just yet.

'I don't know,' said Ivy with a chuckle. 'That politician could do with a good dose _ at least of laxatives!'

Peace fell over Cowagulac.

Chapter 3

Dora was to record her song in Balsham, the nearest town to have any sort of recording studio. Given the technical expertise of Ingrid, her agent, it would have been easy enough to set up her own home studio. However, given the great store everyone was setting on the success of 'I do not entertain the possibility of an interventionist deity but,' Ingrid decided it would look more professional on the credits of the album to have recorded it somewhere other than *Ingrid's garage*. Although Ingrid didn't actually have a garage. She had an old lean-to shed which was living up to its name and leaning precariously against the farm fence.

Ingrid had selected a night recording session, as the rates were much cheaper. Dora complained the entire drive into Balsham.

'How can I be expected to sing at midnight, Ingrid, really? This is too bad, honestly. I'm an *artiste* for goodness' sake. I really don't think I can make a success of this tonight. It's such a difficult song.'

'Dora, my love,' Ingrid didn't glance at her as she drove speedily into the night, ignoring the one hundred kilometres per hour signs, which she considered to be advisory only. 'If you have to record it one note at a time, you will do it. In fact, that might not be such a bad idea.' Ingrid's mind turned to whether it would be possible for the audio technician to grab each note of the scale in tones and semitones, to take the assortment of crotchets and quavers, and put it together like a jigsaw puzzle. The machinery could tweak a note here and there, if one was a bit out of tune. Something to consider anyway. She sounded the horn at a cow which loomed at the side of the road. The noise set the entire herd galloping away from the fence line.

'But Ingrid,' Dora moaned on.

'Enough. I've booked the studio and paid for it, so we are using it and that's all there is to it. Now warm up with some scales, there's a dear. Or you could rehearse that tricky bit in the refrain, you know, where we had to rhyme deity with gaiety.'

Obediently, Dora started some vocal exercises, and Ingrid sang along to encourage her. 'Me me me me me, ma ma ma ma.'

The headlights swept around a bend, and the car swerved over the double lines with enthusiasm. Ingrid corrected the steering wheel and continued the warm-up. 'Silly Sally, shilly shally, seashore swims. Let's sing it as a round, come on.'

Sometime just before midnight, they pulled up outside the studio and got out of the car. Ed, who was the audio tech, moonlighting at this job, had everything already set up.

Dora pulled anxiously at Ingrid's sleeve. 'I don't think I can. I'm scared.'

'Nonsense.'

After being practically dragged inside, Dora sat on a chair in the waiting area, shaking with fear, while Ingrid and Ed checked sound levels, placed stocking filters in front of microphones and ran the backing track. There were no more excuses.

'Up you get, Dora. This could be the start of your music career, you know.'

'Come on, love.' Ed joined in the encouragement. 'You already look the part, you know! Those sparkly things on your jeans really look like something out of *Australia's Got Talent*. Think about how that would look on the cover of the recording.'

Dora smiled. The jeans had indeed been an inspiration, spawned from a video she had seen of *Young Talent Time*. One of the young singers had just such a sequinned arrangement, and by pausing the video, Dora had been able to copy it almost exactly, meticulously sewing each sparkling disc into position. She was equally proud of her faux leather jacket, picked up for a bargain price on eBay. Suddenly she felt confident and strode into the tiny room. Ed swung the heavy doors shut behind her and took up his perch behind the bank of equipment.

Ingrid smiled encouragingly through the glass as she put on some headphones Ed handed to her. 'Can you hear me? Dora, my love, just slip one of those earpieces off, then you can hear yourself sing. Wait for the track, then off you go. Don't worry, Ed will make it sound magnificent.'

Music filled the headphones and Ed slid dials up and down and turned knobs round and round. After a long introduction, the vocals finally began.

Forests, hills or fields of flowers
winter's snows, torrential showers,
sunshine, seas, long summer hours.
Even all your love my darling,
is just seed-husk to a starling
when it comes to changing something
I have told you all along

I do not believe in an interventionist deity, but
don't let that interfere with your delusional holy gaiety.

Wars and bitterness past reason
barely let peace have its season,
speaking justice seen as treason,
do you think that's passed my senses?
Every time a war commences
all your spiritual pretenses
count for nothing in the throng.

I do not believe in an interventionist deity, but
don't think I lack a sense of fun or joy or spontaneity.

Much to Ingrid's surprise, Dora completed a satisfactory recording in just under two hours. Ed ran her off a copy so they could listen to it on the way home.

And listen they did. They played the CD almost all the way back to Cowagulac. Softly, loudly, very loudly, it sounded really impactful. Ingrid was quite overcome, and Dora was buzzing like a bee in a bottle.

'I sound really good, don't I Ingrid? It's all thanks to you, I would never have had the courage to record otherwise, but I think this will be a hit. This will launch me into superstardom! I won't be a boring housewife anymore, I'll be ...' she stopped suddenly.

'What's the matter?' Ingrid wasn't really listening. It was very easy not to listen to Dora. You can only speak so many words in your life and Dora had already spoken a good eighty percent of her quota.

'Oh, Ingrid! I can't let anyone hear this, not until I have a stage name. I mean, whoever heard of a star with a name like Dora Beattie? It sounds like a good name for a cartoon character, or a schoolteacher, or a Rottweiler or something. What am I going to do?'

Ingrid drummed her fingers on the steering wheel. 'I've already thought of that, silly. I've registered your new name; It's Velvet Starshine. I hope you like it.'

Dora clapped her hands and exhaled heavily. 'I love it. It's perfect. It's so *me!*'

She repeated the name under her breath for the rest of the journey, by the end of which Ingrid was ready to strangle her.

Ingrid finally fell into bed at about four in the morning, having gulped down a glass of milk with a chaser of whisky, and slept soundly till nine.

Chapter 4

It was hot. The trees were hanging out for a drink, and the ground around the CCCC was parched and bare. The fledgling garden was wilting, though it revived in the evenings when the watering system from the tank was turned on; just a dribble to conserve the water through the hot months. The workshops were being planned, but everything else was on hold until Ingrid could run the training course.

Despite the heat, Jill's house quite cool, being shaded by verandas on the north and south, while large fans circulated what little breeze came in through the open windows.

Jill was built along generous lines, making her life in summer quite uncomfortable. Her bra and pants stuck to her skin like glue, despite her loose cotton dress. Sweat left uncomfortable wet patches around intimate areas. Droplets rolled down her face, and she sighed as she wiped them away with a moist towelette she had appropriated from a flight to Bali. Her bathroom drawers were packed with tiny bottles of this and that, picked up like a bowerbird from hotel bathrooms, planes and even a restaurant or two. Jill wouldn't ever admit to it, but she had been known to loiter near the maid's trolley at the Bali hotel she had stayed in, and when the coast was clear she had whisked away several plastic shower caps and a couple bottles of L'Occitane shampoo. She justified the theft by reasoning that it was all covered in the hotel's charges, and that, in any case, most people would not be bothered to take the sample-sized bottles. And the shower caps made very handy food covers for leftovers that went in the fridge.

She fanned herself with the local newspaper while flicking through the photo album of her creations on her phone. Ingrid had given her the brief of constructing costumes of Australian animals and birds for Dora. There was seemingly no reason for this, as the song itself had no reference to Australiana, but that wasn't Jill's problem. While not naturally given to self-aggrandisement, she was justifiably proud of her work on Dora's bird costume as well as the other animals she had created for the grand launch of the single. The theme had been a challenge, but she had based the design off a pyjama pattern, then constructed every animal with individual characteristics. Whoever wore the wombat suit had their own sauna, as it was made from fur fabric, but most of the other costumes were at least partly cotton. Despite the fact that she had been cleaning up artificial feathers and cutoffs of fur fabric for the past few weeks, she was pleased with the overall effect of forest life. Here in the country, everyone knew what the animals looked like, so her creations had to be lifelike, and, although the proportions of a human dressed as a koala compared to a human dressed as a possum were illogical, she felt that she had pulled it off.

They had held a dress rehearsal for the launch of Dora's single the previous week. It had taken two hours and a lot of nervous energy, but everyone had been most impressed with the costumes.

'Jill, you've outdone yourself!' Ivy was sincere in her appreciation, and since Ivy was always a remarkably well-dressed lady, Jill took this as a genuine compliment.

Inspired, Jill had replied 'I'm happy to make you a costume too, Ivy. I've always wanted to tackle a crocodile. Would you consider …?' The look on Ivy's face was enough to make her laugh and pretend it was a joke. But Jill was sad inside, as she had been genuine about the offer, and the challenge of the costume would have tested her skills.

At the dress rehearsal, Laura organised the group into their places.

'Rodney, you need to bring in a couple of logs, and make sure they have eucalyptus twigs and leaves. We don't want anything artificial, except for the scent we're spraying. Klaus, make sure you bring some leaf litter in from your place, we can put that in front of the log. And Lancelot, are ready to record the interview? We want it aired on the radio as soon as possible, because a lot of people won't be able to come to the launch. Now, Dora, where are you?' Laura's voice faded into the background as the characters all exclaimed at the sight of each other in full costume.

Bill had set up a sound system, and Dora wanted to run through the song, using the backing track that the studio had made. However, Ingrid put a stop to that.

'No, Dora, I'm not letting you actually sing your song at the launch, so you don't need to practice it today. People can listen to the recording, and you can sign autographs and do as many interviews as you like, but no live singing.' Those nearby could hear her mutter, 'If it comes to that we will deal with it later.'

'But, Ingrid, what about introducing me as Velvet Starshine? If I don't sing, then how will people know my stage name? Everyone here in town knows me as plain old Dora. I have to get the message out that Velvet is a totally different side of me.'

Ingrid put an arm around Dora's waist and led her away from the stage. 'Don't worry, dear Velvet, you'll be famous before long. Now leave all the staging to me and go and get into your cockatoo costume.'

She pushed her out to the bathrooms, Dora protesting in vain, 'But I'm a rosella, not a cockatoo. My costume is red and blue, not boring white and yellow …' Her voice faded into the distance as Ingrid firmly shut the door behind her.

'Right, where's Laura? Laura? Shall we get this show on the road?' A poetry reading from Geranium was to start the program, followed by a talk on extra-terrestrials in the Cowagulac area from Klaus. Then, the grand launch, before a light afternoon tea provided by Rosie as well as the opportunity to buy various dog-oriented artworks from Karen.

Everything was in place. Jill inspected each costume and its wearer, tweaking and pinning where necessary, until she was finally happy with the tableau. The lights were dimmed and Velvet Starshine was introduced by Ingrid, the song played, and everyone applauded generously. Jill smiled to herself, a quiet inner glow as she recalled the comments people had made. Some, who were not locals, had been amazed at the variety and authenticity of the bird and animal costumes, and she was surprised at how well everyone had acted in character as they came out to form the tableau. No one had commented on the relevance of Australian fauna and a song about interventionist deities. Besides, it wasn't Jill's place to worry about such trifles.

***

Finally, it was the day of the launch. Media from the city had been invited, but not many had found themselves able to accept. Nevertheless, the launch was to be covered by the local paper and radio station, and everyone hoped that despite the slightly odd title, Dora's debut recording would bring fame, if not fortune, to the town.

Jill showered for the second time that day, knowing that, before she was even out of the house, she would again be damp with sweat. Muttering about the heat, she walked from the bathroom to the sewing room to the lounge room, picking up needles and cottons, scissors and measuring tapes, pins and patterns and, finally, scraps of every single costume, in case some wardrobe disaster should befall one of the cast members.

Pausing to cram everything into a large, flowery bag, she recalled several disasters in the amateur dramatic circuit which she had been involved with for years. One company had attempted *Turandot*, an ambitious project indeed, and one which nearly ended in disaster. The wardrobe mistress – who was not Jill – had used Velcro on the costume of the Russian Princess as well as that of Prince Calaf. Then, during an ill-fated lip locking stage kiss, the two costumes became inextricably intertwined, Velcro from the dress clinging with more passion than the Princess to the Prince's pantaloons, causing both of them to fall into the orchestra pit. Shortly after that Jill had been called on to replace the Velcro with buttons.

Then, there was *The Merry Widow* season where the yards of trim on one of the cancan dancers' skirts came unravelled and was trailing all the way off stage as heroine Anna tried to fight her way through it. And, of course, there was a myriad of ill-fitting and inappropriate costumes. At least this one would be a triumph of innovation and excellence.

At the CCCC, there was a buzz of excitement. The logs had been hauled into place, the leaves raked into a natural looking semi-circle. The loudspeakers had been disguised by some artfully arranged leafy branches. Only the compère's microphone hit a jarring note. White plastic chairs had been placed in neat rows, and a sumptuous afternoon tea laid out in the kitchen. People started entering, filtering in slowly and universally exclaiming how nice it was 'to get out of the heat.' Jill moved around the offices – which were doubling as dressing rooms – checking costumes. Klaus was heard rustling papers with a sense of importance, and Ingrid stood serenely on stage, looking out over the assembling crowd.

The committee had discussed whether to charge an entry fee for the launch, but it was decided that more people might come if it was free. Several of the ladies had volunteered to cook for the event, while their spouses and children had been coerced into setting out chairs and decorating the hall. Lancelot was acting as chief usher, assisting people to find seats.

'Madam Mayor, welcome to you and your party. C-c-come in, p-p-p-please. I've reserved these seats here, in the f-f-front row for you.'

'Thank you, Lancelot. You've met my nephew and niece,' she said, gesturing to the teenagers accompanying her. 'They are very excited to hear Dora sing. She has quite a reputation, you know.' Onlookers might have queried just how excited the teenagers were, since they had not lifted their faces from their phones.

'Indeed, Madam Mayor. Dora has been on my radio program several times and always gets some favourable c-c-comments. She has led a very interesting life. Speaking of my show, would you consider making a guest appearance?'

'Of course, Lancelot. I'd be happy to come any time. There are so many things in Cowagulac I could talk about. Let's discuss it after the launch.'

Smoothing her suit jacket, she went to take her seat but suddenly jumped up. 'Oh! What's that? Help!' She lurched into the waiting arms of her husband. Karen ran up, trailing a dog-less lead behind her. 'Poochie? Poochie, where are you? Are you all right my little one?' A large wolf hound sized dog had snuck up from behind and laid his snout on the mayor's chair, causing the ruckus. Karen hastily slipped the lead onto his collar and stroked his rough head reproachfully.

'Poochie, what did you think you were doing? You could have got your poor little head crushed, you silly sausage.'

Poochie didn't deign to reply to this comment, merely salivated onto the mayor's chair and lifted his head to gaze at Karen. She dropped to her knees and took his muzzle in her hands.

'Now listen, you. No running away from Auntie Karen. There will be so many people here in a few minutes, and you might get lost. So just stay close to me, okay?' A long tongue snaked out and deposited a layer of slime on Karen's face.

'Thank you for the kiss, my sweet. Now, come with me.'

As Karen disappeared down the aisle, the mayor's husband silently wiped the chair dry, and, without a word, exchanged it with a chair further down the row. The mayor and her party finally sat down, teenage nephew and niece rolling their eyes at each other in a brief pause from gazing in adoration at their phone screens.

Laughter filled the hall as Cowagulac residents, friends and family entered and mingled. Country folk always took the opportunity to make a social occasion out of any event.

Snippets of conversation could be picked out of the hubbub.

'And when the darned magpie swooped me, I was knocked right off my bicycle into the blackberries. I'm sure that dratted bird was cackling in the tree nearby.'

'After my uncle died, you know what he left me in his Will? His GPS! He said I'd lost my way, and this was the only thing he could think of to help me.'

'We need the rain. My dam's near empty and the hay's running out too. Cost me a fortune this year.'

Ivy and Geranium were standing in the aisle, listening. Geranium was taking notes in a small book. When Ivy gave her a sideways look, Geranium explained, 'You never know when it will come in handy. I've got lots of interesting things in this notebook. I'll put them all in a book one day.'

Eventually, Laura bustled up the steps and onto the stage, tapping the microphone. Ingrid cringed, considering it the height of ignorance to tap a quality microphone. Laura called for silence, and the crowd, now over a hundred in number, dutifully obeyed.

'Ladies and gentlemen, esteemed guests, and members of the Cowagulac community, welcome. We are here today to launch one of Cowagulac's little known – as yet – stars.' There was an awkward pause as Laura consulted her running sheet. 'Ms Velvet Starshine.' A smattering of applause followed. 'Ms Starshine is presenting for you her recording of a brand-new song, 'I do not believe in the possibility of an interventionist deity, but.' We will tell you more about this remarkable piece of music later, but to open proceedings, let me call on Geranium Golightly to welcome you with a reading of her poetry. Ladies and gentlemen, please give a warm Cowagulac welcome to Geranium.'

Bowing left and right, Geranium sidled onto the stage and set a small folder on the lectern. Clearing her throat and blinking rapidly, she whispered into the microphone, 'Thank you, I'm honoured to be opening the program today, as I'm new to Cowagulac. I have two poems I would like to read to you. This first one is called 'Bushman's morning.'' The crowd fell respectfully silent.

Dawn breaks with the silence of serenity,
Lambs awaken and plead for mother's milk,
Dingoes slink away to plot and plan for nightfall,
The wind ripples a half-empty dam,
And the bushman awakes.

Jeans and shirt, left on the floor by the bed
As he fell into sleep.
A cold splash of water on his face,
A hearty scratch of his scrotum,
He inserts himself into yesterday's clothes,
Brushes the ants off a hunk of bread, grabbed
From the kitchen for breakfast.

The sun creates a rainbow of colour through the spiderwebs
Trapped on the shed window.
The kelpie waits for instructions, tongue hanging out,
Dripping saliva,
Smiling.
Man, dog, and tractor set out at dawn.
And, in the city, people buy lamb chops on a black plastic tray.

The audience applauded generously, and Geranium took a shy bow. 'My second poem is called 'My Life.''

I was born, I lived, and died.
And now, the Maker is by my side.
Guiding me through the Spirit world
Where all the flags have been unfurled.

Where nations gather, one by one,
Each soul recalling all the fun.
And I am left alone to rue,
Of many deeds, the good were few.

I stole and cheated all my life,
But rarely was involved in strife.
I knew the art of seeming good
Despite being lost in the wood.

But now my spirit guides another
Lesser being, to another mother.
And in this lesson, justly learned,
I'll gain the reward that I have earned.

The applause this time was somewhat muted, one might almost think puzzled. However, Laura made double time to the microphone and asked the audience to give it up for Cowagulac's poet laureate. Perhaps happy to see the end of Geranium, there was a decidedly upbeat feel to the applause. Geranium returned to her seat with a satisfied smile. Ivy squeezed her hand and nodded.

'Now we welcome a special guest, Klaus Fuchs, to speak to us about the UFO sightings here in Cowagulac. Klaus is an expert in all things weird and wonderful.' Klaus shot her an angry look under lowered brows. 'Please welcome our very own interstellar specialist, Klaus.' Laura led the applause, which was enthusiastic from some sections of the audience.

Klaus blew into the microphone and stroked his long, white beard. His strong face was tanned and dramatically weathered. A small beer gut protruded over his trouser line. He was wearing loose jeans, held up with string, and wearing a t-shirt which declared him to be a member of the *Action Alliance Against Alien Abductors*. He cleared his throat and rustled some papers, which he tapped together on the lectern.

'Ladies and gentlemen.' He paused and looked slowly around the expectant faces. 'They *are* here. I have seen them. I know.' There was a murmur among the young men in the back of the crowd. 'In fact, they could be in this very hall, right now. And you wouldn't even know it. Because …' his voice dropped, 'the extra-terrestrials are among us, but they are very cunning. Imagine for a moment that you had landed on another planet. What would its inhabitants think of you? The human is such an odd-looking creature, with a tiny head balanced on a lanky frame, and four appendages extending out at odd angles. Well, that's the situation here.'

Klaus moved his head closer to the microphone. 'Where did I these aliens see? My property is about twenty kilometres from town, out in the sticks. I have for the last forty years there lived. Right from the start, there have been strange lights flashing, regular as clockwork, every three months. But when I go to photograph them,' he paused for effect, 'nothing comes out. Not on film and not on my phone. Nothing, even though the lights are bright enough to plough my crop by.' The audience's faces were arranged into various expressions ranging from fascination to boredom, until Klaus hit the microphone, sending squeals out through the speakers. The crowd winced.

'So how did I come to see them? And why didn't they take me, as so many others are reputed to have been taken? I had on my calendar the dates of every light show, and I decided one night, when the lights were due, to be out there, waiting. I estimated that the lights were about ten kilometres away, so I drove the truck in the direction of the lights, and, on the top of a hill, a watching post I set up. Sure enough, around midnight, the light display started, and, as I watched …' his eyes bulged and watered, and he peered around myopically, 'three figures formed in front of my eyes. The light was shining down, as powerful as a spotlight, but I couldn't see any craft, at least not then. The figures were long and thin, and were covered in a spidery gauze. They glided towards me, and I'm ashamed to say that, on that occasion, I just in the dirt lay face down, shuddering, with my eyes tight shut.'

Now the audience was quiet and entranced. Klaus had them in the palm of his hand with his confession.

'The next time they were due, I went out again to the same place. You might think I was drunk, but I assure you I wasn't. The same experience was repeated, but this time I kept watching. The silvery figures appeared and glided towards me, and on past me, as though I wasn't even there. I felt a chill as they neared, a chill which stayed with me until they disappeared over the hill. I lay there and waited. The night grew cold, but, somehow, I felt warm and comforted. Finally, just as light was about to dawn, two of the figures appeared again. They walked past me, stood in that same spot, and were sucked up into the light. I have experienced first-hand that something is out there.'

Several hands were raised tentatively in the air. 'What happened to the third figure?' A teenager giggled and elbowed his friend.

'That is why I said they might be here in the audience today,' he paused dramatically. 'You see, I never saw the third figure return.' Once more, a hush fell over the audience. Klaus ranged his glance across the crowd. No one moved or even dared to titter.

Klaus stood straight and his tone lightened. 'Laura mentioned astral travelling. That is, I'm afraid something not yet in my field of expertise. However, I can talk confidently about numerology. Those of you who have experienced any difficulties in life, I can assure you that following your numerology profile will give you a better outcome. I am happy to later talk to anyone about this.'

Laura raised her eyebrows and Klaus nodded and moved away from the mike. Laura encouraged another round of applause from the audience. 'Thank you, Klaus, for that most *interesting* talk. I'm sure Klaus will be happy to take questions from you after the performances have finished. But now, ladies and gentlemen, for the moment you have all been waiting for. Let me introduce Ingrid, Ms Velvet Starshine, and the Australian menagerie at the launch of our recording genius.'

Ingrid took a bow centre stage and contemptuously ignored the microphone. 'It has been a real privilege to watch Velvet come out of her shell and record this impressive iteration of her new song. We bring this to you as her world debut, and trust that your purchase of the recording today will support the worthy village of Cowagulac. Velvet appears today in the guise of a rosella, accompanied by the esteemed villagers of Cowagulac, dressed in supportive costumes. These have been made by our own village seamstress, Jill Taylor. Here they come with 'I do not believe in the possibility of an interventionist deity, but.'

The tableau shuffled out on stage and took their positions, posing on the log and in groups, resting fur and feathers on each other.

Finally, Dora was pushed onto the stage by Laura, and there was a hearty round of applause. Ingrid gave a nod to the sound technician, who pressed the play button, and the sound of Dora's voice filled the room, while Dora herself awkwardly stood centre stage, a vision in red and blue, with feathery arms and clawed feet. She held the microphone in her hand, and tried to lip synch the words, but kept forgetting the lyrics, staring out at the audience. Eventually, she gave up the pretence and just stood there.

Despite this, at the end of the music, the applause was generous, and Dora smiled and shuffled forward to take a bow, her large bird feet – gardening gloves sewn to socks – giving her an authentic bird like waddle. Laura took over the mike.

'And please keep that generous applause going for the creator of the magnificent costumes you see here before you today, our very own Jill. She's too shy to come on stage, but I can tell you she has been in the dressing rooms making adjustments right up until the last minute. Even though she won't appear, I'm sure most of you know her, and I'd like to present her with this small gift as a token of our deep appreciation of all her work. Jill, don't forget to collect this before you leave.' Laura smiled and waved a small box in the air.

After that, the formal part of the afternoon had come to an end, with murmurs of congratulations, and a buzz of excitement. Money changed hands as audience members purchased copies of the single, and people flocked to the coffee shop, where a selection of lamingtons, pavlovas, Monte Carlos, lemon slice, as well as cheese and biscuits, had been provided. Some of the out-of-towners made a quick getaway, but a few dozen people lingered, filling cups of tea from the urns until cans of cold beer made their way to the refreshment tables and the hiss of tins being opened cut through the chatter.

The animal costumes had been removed and carefully folded and bagged by Jill, though Dora was reluctant to shed hers. 'Oh no, Jill, I love it so much! I want to keep it on. It might seem silly, but I feel really at home in it.'

Jill smiled, and agreed Dora could have it on as long as she wanted. 'You are the star of the show, after all.'

The red and blue costume could be seen bouncing from group to group among farmers clad in jeans and old sweat stained t-shirts, the mayor and her party in dignified skirts, jackets and suits, and an assortment of husbands and wives in clothes ranging from dowdy to town smart. Ingrid had retired to the dressing rooms, announcing a splitting headache, while Laura was trying to keep the group of young men, who had been the first to tuck into the beer, from hassling Klaus.

'Thank you, young men, I'm sure you have a footy game to go to.' She chivvied them towards the door.

'It's all right, Laura, they want to know about numerology. You know it's a passion of mine.'

Ned, loitering at the edge of the group, snorted derisively. Klaus shot him an angry look.

'I am telling them about the global energy, and how to in their lives harness it. Take young Robert here, for instance.' The group, except for the hapless Robert, sniggered, glad it wasn't them under the spotlight. 'I've looked at his birth number, and some of the significant events in his life. He tells me he has a number of allergies, and I've tried to explain,' he paused and looked earnestly at the young man, whose face was going red and being elbowed by the friends on either side of him, 'that the predominant food he should be eating is carrots. His aura, chakra, and numbers all align around orange vegetables, and, generally speaking, numerology doesn't include pumpkin in its forecasts.'

Laura looked puzzled, but nodded. 'Thank you, Klaus. I'm sure the boys have somewhere to be, don't you, boys?'

They nodded and started edging towards to the door. Klaus continued in their absence, raising his voice as they moved away. 'The unique vibration is a spiritual illumination. Their foundational energy is giving off a sense of deep and profound healing, if they would only stop to adopt the advice I am giving them.' He turned to Laura. 'If they could but bring themselves closer to harmony and balance by mutual respect to the universe showing, they would total spiritual illumination experience.'

Laura took his arm and hooked it into hers, casting a look of entreaty to Ned, who shrugged his shoulders and left. 'Come and have a nice cup of tea, Klaus. Maybe peppermint or camomile, and a little quiche made from farm-fresh eggs and homegrown vegetables. What about that?' Klaus allowed himself to be shepherded to the hospitality area.

'But what is ingredients in the quiche? I normally only eat what I grow myself, then I am totally confident of the nutritional value. You know I am allergic to many foods. And the numbers must be right.'

'Mrs Mellow made the quiches, and Jenny Buttersworth provided the carrot cake. Perhaps you could stick to dry biscuits and cheese, if that would solve the problem.'

'Let me add up. Quiche: seventeen plus twenty-one, plus nine, plus three, plus eight, plus five, no that makes sixty-three, so then that is nine. It must be divisible by two. I can't have quiche.'

Laura stopped in her tracks. 'Well, it's quiche Lorraine, does that make any difference?'

Klaus wrinkled his nose and muttered under his breath. 'Twelve, fifteen, eighteen, ninety-two, forty-six.' He smiled slowly. 'I think I could risk a small slice.'

'I'll go and sort it out,' Laura's voice faded into the background as she disappeared into the kitchen in search of a good feed for Klaus. He was too much skin and bone for her liking.

Slowly, the hall emptied, until finally there were just a handful of ladies washing the cups and packing the remainder of the food into containers. The men would have it served up for morning tea the next day; nothing would go to waste. Laura saw Jill sitting on a wooden chair, staring at the empty stage and fanning herself. She bustled over.

'There you are. Did you get a cup of tea and something to eat?' She sank gratefully into the seat next to Jill and waited for a response. When none was forthcoming, she stole a glance at Jill's face, and though her eyes were closed, her mouth turned up into a small smile.

'Oh, Laura, didn't they look just great? I had no idea how wonderful it would all look together. Just like a walk in the forest, though of course they were much bigger than real animals. But I could just imagine that it was a scene from Klaus's patch of bush, or part of the ranges. It looked so much better than I ever imagined it would.'

Laura patted her hand. 'Indeed, dear, it was magnificent. Now, don't forget your gift. Here it is I hope you like it.' The package was small, rectangular, and beautifully wrapped. Jill took it with tears in her eyes.

'There's no need for a gift, Laura. I was just happy to help.' Nevertheless, she pulled at the ribbon and peeled back the sticky tape. Inside was a silver box containing a shining pair of dressmaking scissors. A grateful tear rolled down her cheek as she hugged Laura and whispered her thanks.

Jill drove home slowly, feeling as though she had eaten one chocolate biscuit too many. Or perhaps two. Next to her on the passenger seat of her ute was the gift, paper loosely wrapped back around the box. *How lovely of Laura to get such a useful gift*, she thought as she turned into the driveway. An unpleasant, blustery north wind was making the shrubs bend and the clothes on the line billow.

'I've got so much sewing to do I'm sure they'll need sharpening before very long.' Jill had gotten into the habit of talking to herself, having lived alone for much of her life. Sometimes, she yearned for the sound of a human voice, and even her own was better than nothing.

Opening the unlocked front door, she dumped her sewing kit on the nearest chair and put the kettle on for a cup of tea. Shedding her loose cotton dress, she stood in front of the fan in her bra and knickers, and raised her arms to dry the sweat patches, standing legs akimbo to get the air into all the crevices. Momentarily, she considered taking off her underwear as well but thought, *at least the cotton catches some of the sweat.*

While the kettle was boiling, she went outside to fetch the clothes off the line. They smelt of sunshine and of the nearby peppermint gum, on which a magpie was sitting, cocking his head at her and warbling a gentle melody. 'It doesn't look like rain, but you can never tell,' she commented. 'It's all very well for you, just a quick dust bath and you're all dinner-suited up.' The bird winked and flew away. She gathered the clothes to her chest, only noticing at the last moment a blob of bird poo on the sheet. 'Oh well,' she mused, wiping it off with a sprig of rosemary, 'it's only on the corner I tuck in.'

With a strong cup of tea and another chocolate biscuit, Jill sat at her lounge room table and examined the scissors. 'My, these are excellent,' she noted as she sliced them through some corduroy fabric that was left over from the echidna costume. 'I'll have to have them sharpened at the shop in town. Can't let them become blunt.'

Heaving herself up off the chair, she padded into the kitchen to make a second cup of tea. Waiting for it to draw, she flicked on the radio, just in time to hear the end of Dora's new song being played on the community radio station. She sighed and smiled at the memories of the day that was.

Chapter 5

Klaus dragged the cuttings of pruned trees towards the centre of his field. Shortly, he would stack them in a pyre and set fire to them. What satisfaction there was in seeing the flames leap up, and smoke billow heavenwards. It was a different sort of smoke altogether than when he smoked his bees and gathered the honey. Or when he got a whiff of smoke from Ned's shed. *That* definitely smelt hallucinogenic.

Once he had gathered twenty-two branches, he paused to catch his breath. His birth number was two, and he associated his destiny with any multiples of this number. He also believed it indicated he was sensitive, balanced, and cooperative, and he tried to live his life that way. As for the constant complaints from his neighbour, Ned (whose birth number was seven and who, consequently, had a volatile personality), Klaus viewed those attributes that Ned found so irksome as a measure of how thoughtful he was – keeping his land free from bushfire fuel, creating harmony in nature by raising bees, and, of course, maintaining constant contact with the afterlife, as signified by his knowledge of the aliens who visited regularly. In addition, he was practising astral travelling. Whenever Klaus involved himself with the number two, he felt a powerful vibration, and knew his soul was being nourished.

He looked across at Ned's property – a mish mash of old tree stumps, logs, broken down chainsaws awaiting repair, and a chicken run with a large, annoying rooster and several submissive hens. And, of course, the vegetable garden. Out of all Ned's property, it was only the vegetable garden which Klaus coveted. His own plot was prone to insect infestation and possum attacks, as well as more mundane problems such as broken irrigation pipes and leaks in the water tank. Ned, on the other hand, had broad beans tall enough to rival Jack's beanstalk, pumpkins of a size to win awards at the Balsham Country Show, and peas that literally burst out of their pods. Klaus knew this because he sometimes sneaked over there at night and inspected them by torchlight. He was determined to get to the bottom of how Ned was able to produce such crops without seeming to spend any time in the garden. *Maybe it's my bees, pollinating all his ruddy plants*, he thought.

Klaus had often noticed Laura's car in Ned's driveway, so he had aired his complaint to Laura. 'What is the secret to his vegetables? I ask but he says nothing. He says he just loves them, and they respond.'

Laura hadn't been much help. 'Maybe it's the sawdust from his carvings,' she suggested. Klaus turned up his lip at such a suggestion and became increasingly irritated at his inability to solve the mystery.

'I must check where his septic tank drains to,' he muttered.

Previously, when he had taken his large torch and crossed over to Ned's garden, he first checked that Ned's van was not in the driveway, and there were no lights on in the house. Once, he had nearly been sprung by Ned, who had been meditating using only a single candle and had come outside to investigate the flashing light.

Ned had opened the door and called out, 'Whoever's there, go away now. The camera's going.' Ned had turned and stomped back inside, and Klaus, who had flung himself lengthwise into the garlic patch, discovered that Ned had recently fertilised the area. Klaus was left with foul smelling, garlic-infested clothes and a lasting impression, burned onto his retina, of a naked Ned.

Other times, when Ned was not home, Klaus moved from bed to bed counting the plants. He firmly believed that the success of the garden had to do with Ned's connection to the number seven. He continued to believe this despite his own plants being in multiples of two and still deriving no benefit.

Klaus licked his finger and held it up to the wind. 'Ha,' he sighed with satisfaction and essayed a small smile. 'The wind should blow the smoke from my honey harvest nicely into Ned's garden.' It wasn't that he hated Ned. Rather, Klaus had come to the conclusion that he was actually jealous of Ned. It had taken several visits to his spiritual advisor before he even accepted this as a working theory. He had tried to speak to Ned about his number seven theory but got short shrift.

'You're barmy, old man. The day you introduce me to your aliens is the first day I will take any notice of what you have to say.'

With that he had swung away from Klaus and pulled the chainsaw rope, causing Klaus to cover his ears and walk away, muttering, 'I'll give them your address, that for certain is.'

Ned often disappeared into his shed for hours, and sometimes, Klaus thought, for days at a time. There was often banging and crashing, along with music blaring through speakers, but Klaus had not had the opportunity to peer inside the shed. On one or two occasions he had sauntered over and knocked on the door, but the only response had been that the music was turned up louder. The windows had been papered over, but electricity ran to the shed, and light leaked through around the edges. He assumed Ned was making modifications to his various branch carving and cutting equipment, though why he should need that many tools was hard to fathom.

Despite Klaus's strong feelings over Ned's garden, there was one thing that Klaus grew to perfection. He was a dab hand at mushrooms. A couple of decades ago, he had started with a little kit in a polystyrene box and was enchanted with the button mushrooms that sprang up. Rather than buying a commercial product, he decided to plant his own, and, after a couple of failed seasons he started to produce excellent crops of a variety of mushrooms. Button mushrooms were perfect, as their number pattern, when reduced to its essentials, was two (ninety-two equals nine plus two, which equals eleven, which equals one plus one, which equals two). Of course, while he would dearly like to grow many varieties, he was limited by their numbers, so while portobellos were excellent (four, which could be divided by two), he couldn't stand growing porcini (three), or morels (five). People were not very understanding of his foibles in this regard, and he had given up explaining. Mushrooms featured in almost all his cooking, so it was fortunate that they were his most successful crop.

***

Safely inside after a night visit to Ned's garden – broad beans were his favourite to visit, as their numbers were forty and twenty-two, both favourable to Klaus, and together they made eight, which was again excellent – Klaus prepared for an evening of alien visitation. These evenings were always marked on his calendar, and, usually, he eagerly anticipated each visit. However, given all the events in the village, he had been too busy to apply himself to the usual preparation. Instead, he downed a quick glass of red wine and a chaser of whisky, inserted a new battery in his lantern and dressed warmly. He started up the old Jeep, put a flask of hot coffee carefully under the seat and headed out, glad his old jalopy didn't make the newfangled *beep* sound if you didn't put your seatbelt on. He had been shopping with Jill once, and the entire way home from Balsham conversation had been impossible with the constant beeps, as the car had labelled Jill's shopping bags as an infant and, therefore, as needing to be belted up.

It was nearing midnight by the time he reached the easternmost edge of the property. He parked overlooking the site of the landing he had witnessed previously. He was no longer excited by the prospect of aliens, except perhaps regarding whether he would be abducted by them, and he didn't feel ready for that. He believed that when the time was right, he would know. Sometimes he wondered if he had been 'taken' and returned to his human body without his knowledge. He decided to discuss this with his therapist at the next opportunity.

After an hour of waiting, the car was cold, and Klaus thought a walk would warm him up. The arrival time of the aliens was unpredictable but was usually not before two in the morning, so he had another hour or so to wait. He quietly let himself out of the car and took a brisk trot to the top of the hill and back. There was no sign of any craft, so he had a cup of coffee from the thermos and settled back with a blanket over his knees to wait.

As the sun rose over the hill and shone onto his face, Klaus awoke with a start. How could he have fallen asleep? Who knows what might have happened when he was dead to the world? Shaking with a combination of anger and distress, he took a leak at the nearby eucalyptus and opened the thermos. To his surprise, it was empty. *I'm sure I only had one cup*, he mused. *Ah well, maybe I didn't fill it up. I'd better be home getting and a real cup of hot coffee making*. He drove right to the edge of the hill but couldn't see any markings where a craft might have landed during the night. He was reassured. As his brain started working properly, he banged his fist on the steering wheel. 'Agh! That's why they didn't come. It's the seventeenth. Not divisible by two. Not my night.' Much relieved, although slightly perturbed he had put the wrong date in his calendar, he drove quickly over the bumpy track, catching a couple of hours more sleep before beginning another day. The next night would be far more suitable.

This time, waiting till midnight, Klaus had time for a nap before setting out. He drank only water, avoiding both alcohol and coffee. Much to his disappointment, there was again no sighting.

He made a new plan for the twentieth, which had the advantage of being not only divisible once by two, but was also a simple number with a two and a zero. Regarding this as an omen, Klaus rose early on that day, intending to take a calming walk in the fields closest to the possible alien craft landing site. Buckling up his gaiters, he gathered his walking stick, binoculars and a book of mantras that he was practicing. Holding the book in one hand he walked slowly through the knee-deep grass, muttering to himself as he forced the stalks aside. It was tiring, though, and he stopped after the first paddock and hoisted himself onto the fence post.

As he gazed over the field, he noticed something was amiss. Bringing the binoculars to his eyes, he slowly swung them across the grass. 'Well, I'll be damned.' He swivelled the binoculars back to where he started and swept them across the field again. A cloud of whiteflies flew into his mouth, and he realised it had fallen open. He spat several times, then closed his lips tightly. Jumping off the fence post, he strode towards the field, extracting his mobile phone as he went. Sure enough, there was an indentation about two metres from the start of the grass. He turned and followed it, photographing on his phone as he went. At one stage, he knelt and sniffed the ground. 'Nothing,' he muttered, 'but it should smell.' The stalks were broken, and it looked almost like they had been burned. 'I need a vantage point. I want to see this from above. I'm sure there's a pattern, maybe a message.' The more he thought about it the more excited he became. 'In the two nights I didn't come out, *they* have visited! They carved out my very own crop circle. Surely people will believe me now. Unless they put it down to a stunt. Where's the highest point? I must look over the field from above.'

The foothills of Mermaid Mountain were too far away, but there was a slight rise only three hundred metres away, and Klaus could hear the sound of a tractor in that direction. Hurrying around the outskirts of the field, he found his neighbour, Harry, ploughing, and after a shouting match in which neither man could understand what the other was saying, Harry turned the tractor off, and Klaus found himself yelling into the silence.

Harry wasn't all that happy about stopping work, but reluctantly agreed to let Klaus stand on the roof of the tractor. 'Only for a moment, mind. I've got work to do, even if you don't.' Without hesitation, Klaus climbed up, and from the top was able to take some snaps of the field. Hardly pausing to thank Harry, Klaus hurried home and downloaded the photos to his computer. The ones from the tractor were quite spectacular, depicting a circular design, with criss-crosses at regular intervals. Klaus sat back in his office chair, stunned. Crop circles! What next? Surely a visitation. It was a sign.

Chapter 6

'Spider! Sausage! Ringo!' Karen called the roll of her dogs, and they bounded up to her, licking, barking, and jumping. 'Such a noisy lot, you are.' Karen patted their rough heads in turn, making sure each received the same amount of attention. Her favourite, Whisky Darling, was hanging back a little and, when she noticed this, Karen pushed the others away and knelt to put her arms around him. He was such a large dog that his nose was almost level with hers. 'What's up with my schnookums, then? Eh? Is my smoochie woochie all upset about something?'

Now that he had her undivided attention, Whisky Darling let out a foul-smelling burp and complemented it with a silent, but deadly, fart. Karen wrinkled her nose and stood up.

'Okay, dinner. Come on, you lot.'

The dogs all bounded out to the kitchen, where their labelled bowls were laid out on paper on the floor. As she prepared their individual dietary supplements, Karen hummed her favourite tune, 'How Much Is That Doggie In The Window?' and added the barks herself. Spider tilted his head to one side as though trying to work out whether she meant to sell them. As much as she adored Whisky Darling, she thought Spider was the most intelligent.

Dinner over, the dogs settled in front of the television, while Karen laid out her oil paints to continue the latest portrait in the series *Hairy Hounds*, which she hoped to display as an exhibition later in the year. She had already finished two, and, with her speedy palette knife technique – which Laura had once referred to hurtfully as 'slapdash' – she anticipated finishing the portraits of her own dogs in a couple of weeks, before calling in other dogs from the Wolfhound Association.

The picture she was working on was of Ringo, the smallest of her brood. He had a hairy fringe which seemed to part in the middle, the long hair dangling over his eyes. Karen tenderly smoothed it away and ran her hands over his shaggy coat. 'You could do with a good bath and brush, young fellow,' she murmured. He acknowledged the comment with a wag of his feathery tail before collapsing on the floor, reluctantly sitting up when Karen called his attention to the pose she required. He patiently crossed his front paws and looked straight ahead, as though a trained model. 'I do love the way you smile at me.' Karen mixed some grey and black and slathered it onto the canvas.

An hour later, she sighed and laid down her palette knife.

'I think that's done. Any more and it would be spoilt.' She turned the picture around. 'Have a look, Ringo, and tell me what you think.'

Ringo, now off duty, was laying on the floor, ribs heaving, saliva drooling from his open mouth. Reluctantly, he lifted his head, barked gently, and laid down again. Whisky Darling trotted over and laid his head on her knee.

'Sweetheart,' she murmured, 'I'm so glad I have you. Who needs a man, eh? That silly sister of mine, she's nuts over Ned. I ask you, why would you want to have a relationship with a man who cuts his bread with a chainsaw?' Whisky Darling licked her hand in reply, then turned tail and headed to the bedroom. 'Okay, I'm coming. You go ahead.'

By the time Karen had brushed the dogs and bedded them down, it was well after ten, and she took a cup of warm milk with her to the bedroom, where Whisky Darling was already sprawled out on top of the sheet. The night was hot, and little air stirred. As she slowly undressed, a refined snore issued from Whisky Darling, and he quivered as some doggy dream took hold. Karen stood in her cotton nightie, looking at him, a faint smile on her face. 'Now, my pretty, is it worth the trouble to move you?' Whisky Darling didn't deign to reply. Karen considered the enormous physical effort in shoving the dog to one side, then thought how hot the sheets would be. Sighing, she quietly picked up her book from the bedside table and made her way to the spare room, closing the door gently so as not to wake the dog.

By six the next morning, the house was alive with the clamour of dogs demanding walks and breakfast, not necessarily in that order. Karen jumped out of bed and dressed hastily before opening the back door to the tribe and preparing their breakfast while they were completing their trips to the toilet. All except Whisky Darling, that is, who stood at the kitchen door, glaring at Karen from under lowered brows. Turning, she caught sight of him and jumped.

'I'm sorry, my sweet, but you were fast asleep, and I didn't want to wake you. I missed our cuddles, of course. Come here and we will have one now.' But his four paws stood firm, and, for once, Karen didn't give in. 'Very well then, here's your breakfast.' She held the plate out and, for ten seconds, it was touch-and-go before the dog conceded and came forward to lick and sniff Karen's hand. 'All is forgiven. All is right in the world.' Her eyes misted over.

The morning light revealed that the portrait of Ringo needed a little more work, so she sat on the arm of the chair and made some adjustments before reluctantly getting out the vacuum cleaner. The amount of hair shed by the dogs filled the vacuum bag several times over, but she had the house to herself because they all hated the noise of the machine, and none would enter while it was operating. As much as she loved her dogs, she secretly enjoyed these rare moments of solitude.

Chapter 7

Laura sat smiling dreamily into the distance, a look of peace and hope softening her round, plump face. She pined for her hero. Surely he had noticed how she admired his artistic, manly skill with the chainsaw, hanging on every word he delivered on matters of natural history and bush skills, adoring his rough charm and idiosyncrasies of speech. If only he would just once meet her gaze. Especially enticing was the way his tattoos rippled as his arms moved, making them appear alive. The big butterfly – or maybe moth – on his right forearm held particular fascination. She was fast running out of reasons to call on Ned, and this had even been commented on by that odd Klaus, who lived next door. After all, to drive twenty kilometres into the country one really did need a valid reason. Laura had delivered Ned a personal invitation to all the village activities she had tried to start, but Ned was not only uninterested, he had also been quite speedy in refusing to participate.

'Ned …' she whispered his name out loud with a big sigh, then looked nervously back at the upturned jam jar she had placed on the sideboard. It would please Ned, she thought, to be consulted on matters of identification, picturing his pleasure and fascination when her offering caught his eye. She thought she had been very brave to capture such a handsome specimen, with its round black body and bold red stripe, not at all like the huntsman she had cohabited with in the living room these last few weeks, or the common daddy long legs in the bathroom.

She had only to take the next step. She had been attracted to Ned for months but had barely exchanged more than the simplest of conversation. He was no wordsmith, but there was something about him that made her heart beat faster.

All the way to Ned's house, her thoughts ricocheted between the nightmare of her captive escaping and her daydream of Ned's first prickly kiss, his rough facial hair scraping against her face. Unsurprisingly, it was the thought of the kiss that most impacted on her driving abilities, and she narrowly missed the elaborately carved post – a hovering blowfly – that marked the entry to Ned's place.

She stopped a while at some distance from the house, but close enough to watch Ned at work on his latest creation – whether mermaid or centaur was unclear at this stage – nervously glancing at her specimen in the jam jar every few seconds. At last, she drove closer. Stepping out of the car, she cradled the jar behind her back.

'Hello, Ned?' she called. 'Ned?' He was too engrossed to hear her, or perhaps it was the buzz of the chainsaw washing out any human sound. As Laura approached, he continued his work, before finally looking up, with a quick nod in Laura's direction.

She waited patiently, even reverently, for him to pause.

'How can I help you, Laura?' he asked at last, chainsaw still running. 'Good to see you— 'scuse me another few seconds will you, please?'

'Oh, I don't need anything thank you Ned – I just wanted to consult you about something,' Laura said shyly, withdrawing her gift from behind her back, but still clutching it close. Ned was working on a wing of some sort, clearly engrossed in every last feather's detail. A griffin perhaps?

It was only then that Laura noticed something different about the spider.

It wasn't moving any more. Sitting with its legs curled up, it looked so much smaller. It looked, in fact, dead.

Laura did her best not to burst into tears, filled with remorse that she hadn't thought about making sure there was enough air for the poor creature – why else would it have died?

'Ned, I'm so sorry, I had a lovely spider specimen to show you, but it's died already,' she almost sobbed. 'Perhaps you could tell me more about it anyway? Add it to your collection?' Above the noise of the chainsaw, she wasn't sure if Ned heard, but he did give the jar a sideways glance. Encouraged, Laura proceeded to open the jar, intending to deliver the dead spider to Ned's anticipated palm. She waited with the spider in her own hand until she could catch his attention again.

The spider spread all eight of its legs abruptly and began to crawl up her arm. Laura leapt in fright, flinging the spider at Ned's feet. He started, and lost control of the chainsaw, which continued to rotate, swinging up towards his head, his eyes widening as the blade approached before slicing almost the whole way through his neck at the jugular. Laura screamed, first in shock, then in pain, suddenly aware that the spider had bitten her bare foot. Within seconds, she had fainted across Ned's bleeding body.

***

The chainsaw was still running circles in the dust, dangerously close to Laura's head, when Klaus pulled up a short while later, finding two bloodied bodies, only one still moving – and moaning. Laura had hit her head on the half-finished, ill-fated sculpture when she fell, and was concussed.

Klaus scanned the bloody path, noting the spatters on the nearby bushes and soaked into the crevices of the half-finished piece of wood. He gingerly approached the chainsaw as it danced around in unpredictable circles. He stood for a moment and watched it, trying to discern a pattern. This was a small chainsaw, which Ned usually used for the fine cuts on his sculptures, more like a lethal variety of hedge trimmer, and Klaus had to look closely to decipher how to make the machine stop. He cursed Ned and his constant modifications to his tools. Every other chainsaw would have stopped the moment the hand was off the trigger but, no, Ned had to have things exactly as he liked them.

Another groan from Laura prompted him to take action. He darted into the centre of the circle and grabbed the handle, his fingers narrowly missing the blade, which enabled him to press the 'stop' button. The silence was deafening. He ran to Laura, frantically trying to remember his first aid training.

'Laura, can you hear me?' He shook her by the shoulder (page 5 of the first aid manual). She groaned and he was relieved, knowing he wouldn't have to do CPR. He rolled her over on her side, (recovery position, page 8), and phoned triple zero.

'Which service do you require?'

'Ambulance. There's been a terrible accident. Main Road, Cowagulac.'

'Stay on the line please, caller.'

Klaus dropped the phone on the dirt and listened to the squawking from the tinny loudspeaker. He yelled the answers to the questions as they were fired at him.

'Laura, and Ned, those are the people who are in trouble.' Indistinct mutterings from the phone.

'Looks like a chainsaw ran amuck. Ned, he's a chainsaw artist. How long will this ambulance be?'

Laura groaned, and Klaus turned his attention to her again. 'It's okay Laura, the ambulance is on the way, just stay still.'

'Ned?' her voice whispered.

'Don't worry about anything, just stay still.' (Page 15, reassure the patient)

The sound of a siren came within earshot and a relieved Klaus got up off his knees and looked around intently.

After the ambulance pulled up, two officers in crisp uniforms speedily absorbed the situation, and, while one attended to Laura, the other confirmed that Ned was dead. He went over to his colleague.

'I don't know what happened here, but we better call the police.'

Klaus caught the word, and his heart leaped, as though he had done something wrong, even though he was the innocent bystander. A sedan pulled up and another ambulance officer emerged, who was quickly updated by one of the first two, while the other pulled the gurney out from the ambulance. 'We need to take the woman to hospital,' the first officer said. 'Simon here will help with organising the deceased.' She gestured to her colleague.

'Are you okay?' Simon looked anxiously at Klaus, as though trying to calculate what he could do if he had to fit two patients into the vehicle, but Klaus smiled and nodded.

'I'm fine, just a bit shaken.'

Laura was loaded into the ambulance, which pulled out of the driveway, siren blaring, leaving Simon and Klaus standing there. Klaus had no idea what to say but Simon directed the conversation, taking meticulous notes in tiny handwriting in a notebook with an official-looking leather binding. 'What can you tell me about the gentleman there?'

Klaus looked away, the red stains a vivid reminder of the violent way in which Ned had died.

'I live next door and often keep an eye out for Ned's property. He is notoriously careless about leaving his house open, and I don't want any chance burglar to decide to start on my place after ransacking his. I was driving past, on my way home, and saw a body on the ground. I pulled up – that's my Jeep out there – and this was the scene that I saw.'

'Not what you might expect, sir. What did you say your name was?'

'I didn't. But it's Klaus.'

'Thank you, sir. What did you do when you got out of the car?'

'First thing was to turn off that chainsaw. Making a dreadful racket it was. That took me a few minutes, because it was going round in circles, and I didn't want to cut my own leg off. Then I saw to Laura, got her on her side, and called you lot. And that's really all I can tell you.'

A swirl of dust indicated another car had arrived, this time the police. Constable Makepeace, who had probably imagined a country town posting would consist of an odd tractor theft and the occasional drunk making trouble, must have been thinking he should have opted for a city station. He paled when he saw the bloody scene in front of him, but with his Sergeant climbing out of the passenger seat, he had to keep moving.

Once again, Klaus repeated his story, though, since he knew the constable, he added in a hiss under his breath, 'It was the aliens, you know. Ned was too savvy to be caught in such a way. He lived and breathed that bloody chainsaw, and I should know because I heard it all day, every day. The only way he would have stuffed up would have been alien intervention.'

Makepeace was not sure how to respond and was relieved that his Sergeant came over at that moment and he was able to move away. Klaus was an unnerving character. Always intense. Always serious.

The sergeant asked for the same details again, and Klaus lost his temper. 'Look, I live next door. I've told this story three times now. If you want anything more, come over to my house. I'm going home for a brandy and a cup of tea. These people were friends of mine. If I'm right – and I am – I need to be out tonight looking for the aliens who did this.'

He turned and stalked back to his ute, slamming the door and speeding away dramatically. The sergeant looked at Makepeace, who rolled his eyes and shrugged.

'Bit of a character, sir. Well known to be slightly on the barmy side.'

'Not exactly how we would describe it in a report though, is it, Constable?'

'No, sir.'

'Just how would you describe it in your report?'

Makepeace pulled his ear tentatively. 'The witness reported that he believed the event—'

'Incident.'

'Sorry, sir. The witness reported that he believed the incident was caused by alien intervention,' he sounded the last word out in all its syllables.

'Good. And what do you think of that possibility?'

The two officers walked around Ned's body, examining it from all angles, though Makepeace looked away more than he looked at the body.

'Don't think it's very likely myself, sir. Klaus has often talked about alien visitation, so I've no doubt he believes it.'

The sergeant stooped and peered closer at the gaping neck wound, around which the blood had dried in the hot sun. 'Ever seen them yourself, lad?' The sergeant didn't look up, so didn't see the fleeting expression of fear and surprise which crossed Makepeace's face.

'No sir. That is … no. Never.'

The sergeant was distracted by waving away the blowflies which had swarmed around the ragged wound edge, and stood up, dusting his knees. 'I have. Better get this chap photographed and off to the morgue. Have you got the camera?'

'I use my phone, Sarge. It's high quality.' Makepeace dreaded taking the photos, as they stayed on his phone until they were submitted to the coroner, and he had been known to inadvertently show his friends crime scene photos when he was looking for the ones of his cavoodle, Leila, much to their amusement. He resolved to download these to the office computer the moment he finished at the scene.

'Looks like it's just an accident at any rate. After you've taken the photos, shoot off to the office and start writing the report, would you? I'll see about getting this chap to the morgue.'

Makepeace was only too grateful to have this program laid out for him, despite the prospect of having to drive many kilometres back to the office then no doubt return to pick up his boss. After snapping a few pictures of the general scene and some closeups of the wound, he departed, leaving the sergeant to deal with the body, the aliens, and Klaus.

For the whole drive back to the station he kept remembering *that* weird experience he had when he was a kid. It was not aliens, he reassured himself. No doubt. His parents had dismissed the idea of creatures from outer space and put it down to too much cheese with the pasta. All the same … he hadn't forgotten it, even twenty years later. The sergeant's offhand 'I have' comment reverberated in his mind.

Meanwhile, the ambulance had deposited Laura at the hospital, where she was x-rayed and inspected for injuries. Once the blood, which had saturated her clothes, had been cleaned, and the concussion diagnosed, she was left in peace and, before long, was asking for 'a cup of tea and possibly a sandwich, because I missed lunch.' An obliging nurse produced not only tea and a sandwich, but also a chocolate muffin, which all made Laura feel significantly chirpier, though every time she thought about Ned, she felt like bursting into tears.

Although Laura tried to talk to them, the other ladies in the ward were non-communicative. One bed appeared temporarily empty, one was occupied by an elderly lady who was sitting out in her chair, and the third was occupied by a woman who had gigantic headphones on, through which Laura could hear the canned laughter of the TV show she was watching.

The sides of the bed had been pulled up and Laura was unable to get out, so she rang the bell for assistance. 'What if I needed to go to the toilet?' She spoke out loud but got no response. After pressing the bell several more times the obliging nurse came in, but said Laura couldn't leave the bed till the doctor had visited her.

'And when is that likely to be?'

'Doctor generally does his rounds just before dinner. He should be here soon.' She made a note on the chart at the end of Laura's bed and disappeared out the door while Laura was still forming her next question.

Using the handrail to haul herself to a sitting position, she hit her foot on the cot railings. She squealed and threw the covers back. A red swelling had developed on her foot, which was now throbbing. She pressed the bell again, and when the nurse arrived, she showed her.

'I think this is a spider bite. I remember now, the spider bit me after I shook it out of the container and it came to life. Oh, what if it's here in the bed with me?' She frantically waved the sheets in an attempt to dislodge any lurking insects.

'It's okay, miss.' The nurse tried to calm Laura. 'You've been showered, you're in a hospital gown, and the bed has clean sheets so there's no way a spider could be in there keeping you company.'

Laura relaxed and stopped pulling at the sheets. 'Of course, you're right. But I have to show the doctor this bite. I might be poisoned. The spider had a red stripe.'

The nurse nodded. 'I'll ring the doctor for advice. Just stay put and keep calm.' She scurried out, and Laura could hear her at the nurses' station just outside her room. She started to feel dizzy and a little nauseous and hoped she wouldn't vomit the sandwich and muffin back up. Before that could happen, she fainted, and when she came to, sometime later, it was to a foot that was bandaged professionally, and the nurse from earlier sitting by her side.

'It's all good. The doctor had a look and has given you a shot of anti-venom for redback bites. He's pretty sure that's what it was, and you're stable now. But he wants you to stay in hospital for the next couple of days so we can monitor things. You have quite a severe concussion, too. You must have had quite the shock.'

Laura considered the options. It was extremely pleasant to be looked after and cossetted, but she had so many things to be going on without her there. And Ned. Poor, poor Ned. Well, maybe just a day or two in bed wouldn't hurt. Suddenly feeling very tired, she nodded her head and dozed off.

***

The next day she felt much better and was able to consume juice, scrambled eggs, toast, cereal, and a fruit platter for breakfast before the sergeant arrived to take her statement. Once again, she had to re-live the event, and Constable Makepeace soon brought her statement back to the hospital for her to sign.

'Please read it first, miss, so I can make any changes that are necessary.'

She scanned it as fast as her still aching head allowed, reading it aloud.

'My name is Laura, and I live at an address known to the police. I took a spider in a jar to Ned, as he was an expert in spiders, and I knew he would be able to identify it for me. When I got out of the car, he was working with his chainsaw on a sculpture. I went up to him, but he didn't hear me approach. To my horror, I saw that the spider in the jar was dead, so I tipped it out onto my hand so I could show Ned. Then the spider came to life, and I screamed and dropped the jar and the spider, and frightened Ned. He let go of the chainsaw and it went flying up in the air and suddenly there was blood everywhere and he was on the ground. I fainted and hit my head on the sculpture. The spider must have bitten me on the leg. I now know it was a red back spider.'

She looked up. 'And Ned, is he dead?' She knew he must be because he couldn't have lived with such a wound. Makepeace nodded gravely, and Laura found the tears pricking her eyes.

'I love him. And he loved me too. Or, he would have loved me, in time.' Only the arrival of her lunch finally quelled the tears.

After lunch was polished off, Laura started to feel hot and bothered and, worse still, slightly nauseous. It had been a tasty casserole of chicken, followed by steamed pudding with fruit. Swallowing hard on a potential bubble of vomit, she pressed the bell for the nurse.

'I feel a bit sick,' she announced to the ward, in the absence of the immediate attention of the nurse. No one responded, and she called out, her voice quavering.

'Nurse! I feel sick.' She started sweating and wiped her forehead with the sheet.

Through blurred vision she saw the nurse arrive and felt a great sense of relief. 'I'm not well,' she managed.

'Looks like a temperature. Hold still while I measure it.' The nurse held a gadget to her ear, then shook her head.

'I'll get the doctor to look at you. Just rest, dear.'

Laura tried to rest but wasn't particularly successful. She was in a great deal of pain. Fortunately, it wasn't long before the doctor was examining her and prescribing a course of antibiotics and some pain relief. But by evening, she wasn't feeling much better, and though she spooned up some spicy tomato soup, she couldn't even make a start on the roast lamb and vegetables, let alone the pavlova. This was difficult for Laura, who hated wasting food, but she didn't have the energy to eat, and the thought of food made the nausea return.

***

The tablets she had been given must have assisted in knocking her out, as she spent a dreamless night fast asleep, despite not having had dinner.

The next morning, though, the swelling in her foot had increased and the bandage felt tight around it. The nurse who had checked on her during the night frowned as she examined it and snapped on a new pair of plastic gloves before she removed the bandage. A dressing trolley was wheeled in, and Laura felt some sort of liquid being applied to the wound, followed by another dressing. Laura felt limp and unable to participate in any banter with the nurse, or even to attempt a chat with the other inhabitants of the ward.

Once alone, Laura examined her foot curiously. It felt sore, and she wondered how long the bandage would have to stay on. *What a nuisance it will be when I'm doing housework or gardening,* she thought. Looking around surreptitiously, she unhooked the bandage clasp and slowly unwound the dressing. Eventually, she reached the end and gently lifted the pad covering the bite. She noted the swelling, the redness, and felt an almost uncontrollable urge to itch the site. She was peering at her leg more closely when, suddenly, she became afraid of the nurse arriving to find her unbandaged. She hastily reattached the pad and wound the bandage back as best she could.

After her cup of tea – and two sweet biscuits, as the lady opposite didn't want one – she lay back, still feeling feverish. The nurse came and changed the bandage again, tutting about the amount of blood which had gathered and spread through the dressing and the covering. A nurse she hadn't seen before came in and took her temperature, made some notes on the chart, and hastily left the ward.

Another hour or so later, a couple of orderlies arrived, unhooked her bed from its moorings and started to wheel her away.

'What's happening?' Laura thought she asked, but since they didn't respond she started to worry that she only spoke in her head, but, soon enough, a nurse addressed Laura.

'We're just taking you to another ward, love. You need a bit more care than you can get here.'

Laura didn't feel very comforted by this and tried to ask again what was happening. The words came out jumbled and sounding as though she was drunk.

'We're just popping you into IC for a day or two, so we can monitor you better, okay?'

Laura wondered what IC was, and in a muddle-headed way went though some possibilities. *In care? Incarceration? Maybe they will lock me up? Or maybe it means incompetent?* She giggled at the last one, but a shiver went through her as the more likely meaning came to mind. *Intensive care.*

Did that mean she was going to die? Should she write a new will? Had she even written an old will? What would happen to her estate? The thoughts started whizzing around and made her dizzy. Mercifully, she found herself sleepy and drifted off.

When she awoke, it was dark outside. She could see the reflections of streetlights and heard cars whizzing by as though on a wet road. Cowagulac didn't have any streetlights, and it took her a few moments to work out she was in Balsham Hospital. A rumbling stomach suggested to her that she hadn't eaten for a while, and the first thing she said to the nurse who came to check her temperature was,

'Can I have something to eat?'

The nurse smiled, and her eyes twinkled. 'I'm glad to see you have your appetite back. We were getting a bit worried about you. I'll organise some sandwiches but let me check that bite first.' She unwound the bandage and nodded approvingly. 'Now that's looking much better. Good girl.'

She turned to leave the room, but Laura, having been approved of, called out, 'Could I have tomato and cheese, please? With mayo. And a cup of tea.'

The next couple of days saw her strength return quickly, and she was moved back to a non-intensive ward. There was only one other inhabitant, and they had some amicable chats before the other lady was moved out, and Laura had the room to herself.

Several days passed quickly, with all the activities of the hospital along with the visitors she had.

Ivy and Geranium came to visit, then Klaus, Karen and Lancelot. It was only when she was alone that she remembered Ned, and felt sad.

***

Once she was on the mend, Ivy told her what had been happening. She had called in to visit one afternoon, pulled out some knitting, and made herself comfortable in the visitor's chair. 'You caused quite a stir, young lady,' she began. 'This bite of yours turned into an infection that managed to circulate itself through the hospital.' She saw Laura try to sit up and put up her hand to stop her. 'It's nothing to do with you, don't worry about that. It was the way it all happened. You suffered the bite and the pain, so don't you go worrying about the aftereffects. It's about time the hospital had a shake-up of their procedures.'

'But how bad was it? I missed it all.'

'It started off with one or two people getting a mild staph infection, but, before long, it had rampaged its way through most of the wards. They had a deal of trouble getting it under control, but it's all fixed now.' Ivy smiled and picked up her knitting again. 'No need for you to worry. We have been waiting for you to get better before we discuss Ned's funeral.' She saw Laura's bottom lip quiver. 'I don't mean to upset you, love, but it has to be arranged.'

'I feel so bad. If I hadn't taken him the spider, he would still be alive. It's all my fault.' She felt the tears gather and let herself enjoy the drama of it all a little bit. After all, she never got had a real relationship with Ned, except in her mind.

'It's all right, Laura. His relatives arrived and arranged a cremation, but they have agreed to wait till you are fit again before the scattering of the ashes.'

***

After Ivy had left, Laura felt the need to be out of the hospital and back in the community. Goodness knows what they were doing without her to run things. She pressured the doctor into releasing her, claiming that she felt much better and couldn't stay any longer, taking up the valuable bed space.

'I'll only let you go if you promise to stay at home for another few days. I'll arrange a visiting nurse to check on you, so make sure you don't overexert yourself.'

After a final lunch of crumbed veal with vegetables, sticky date pudding, and two cups of tea, Laura signed out of the hospital and took a taxi home.

Ned's death seemed to have cast a pall over the whole village. Laura felt a different vibration to the rhythm of Cowagulac. Everyone seemed to be spending more time in their houses. Activity at the CCCC was muted. She called in at the shops, and tried to make conversation, but was met with short answers and no encouragement to pursue gossip.

'What's been happening while I was sick?' she asked the newsagent.

'Same as usual. People come. People go.'

'I was out of it, in intensive care, in pain.'

'Bad luck, then, weren't it.' And that was all she could get from him.

It wasn't much better at the bakery, though she did go at peak bread-buying time and the shop was busy. After trying a couple of friendly lines with no response, she turned on her heel and left – though reluctantly, as the eclairs looked especially tasty, glistening with thick chocolate icing and oozing with cream.

After all I do for the community, you'd think I deserved a bit of sympathy, she thought. *But I suppose they blame me for Ned's death.* The thoughts set off a chain reaction and only a couple of bars of chocolate could comfort her.

Chapter 8

Meanwhile, Jill, without anywhere else to go, contemplated her next project. She had long believed that Ned's chainsaw sculptures, while being all very well in their own way, hardly reflected the diversity and creativity of the village. She had heard – though Ned had never admitted it – that he had been given a large grant by either the local Arts Organisation or the Chainsaw Artists Guild, to create the monstrosity that was *Surf's up at Cowagulac*. She had never understood the humour of depicting surf in the middle of country Victoria, and it seemed a ridiculous waste of time and energy. Besides, Ned didn't seem the type to have such deep and insightful philosophy as to project an irony such as this. Jill's planned murals, on the other hand, to be painted on the sides of buildings, would be a pleasant refreshment for the eye of tourist and local alike. In fact, they might attract tourists, who usually sped through Cowagulac on the way to somewhere else. Of course, it was distressing that Ned was gone, but it did clear the way for her own art to come to the forefront.

Initially, there had been some resistance from Karen, whose dog sketches were apparently known throughout, well, maybe a circumference of some twenty kilometres. Karen had mentioned vaguely that perhaps they could work in concert, with dogs being included in all the murals, but Jill had a totally different idea. She would be painting enormous pictures of the locals, including the weatherbeaten, craggy Klaus, the elegant, newly arrived Ivy, the chubby Laura – Jill herself knew enough about slabs of fat and overhanging belly to be able to accurately draw these shapes and just add Laura's head on top. She would draw Rosie behind the café counter, Lancelot with his headphones on and mike at his mouth. It was all a very exciting and challenging prospect. Ned would feature too, to show there was no ill-will towards his art, and as a fitting memorial to him. She had already made a number of sketches, and all that was needed was the go-ahead from the owners of the buildings and approval from the council. She had filled in all the forms, but it was now a waiting game, and she was anxious to get started. With any luck, she had put Karen off the idea by asking her to contribute half the money.

She was frustrated, though, by being required to buy the paint. She was happy to donate her services, even to bring the ladder and brushes in her ute and set them up – she had every intention of disobeying the *no ladders over age fifty* advice, since this would be on a level surface, and, in any case, her balance was incredible. She calculated the paint would cost over a thousand dollars, and she couldn't imagine any way to recoup the money. Possibly, other villages might want to emulate the idea, and engage her services, but it was by no means certain. However, she was prepared to do the first one anyway and see what developed from there. In fact, she had permission from one of the building owners to begin, and after the stress of the launch, coupled with Ned's dramatic death, she decided to go ahead with it.

In this mural, she planned to depict the villagers, with smaller portraits of the main village characters in the CCCC. Lancelot was at the lectern, Laura hovering in the background. Rosie was handing coffee to Ivy, while Klaus, holding a basket of mushrooms, was deep in conversation with Ned, whose long hair was draped over his shoulder. Karen was hugging a dog. Depicting Klaus actually conversing amicably with Ned was definitely the result of some artistic licence.

What Jill didn't take into account was her ability, or lack thereof, to inoffensively caricature the people she was drawing. In keeping with the best cartoonists, she picked out a big nose here, a birth mark there, thinning hair or thick spectacles. All these idiosyncrasies were liable to give offence, especially once magnified on a large brick wall. When Jill looked at her work, however, all she felt was a sense of pride.

It took her a couple of days to garner her energy and collect the paraphernalia required. She had sketches ready, drawn into a grid, and on Tuesday morning she drove off, fully equipped, ready to begin. The wall was already whitewashed and primed, so Jill set up two ladders and a board between them, selected the charcoal to draw the outlines, and began.

Engrossed in her work, with a portable radio tuned to her favourite country music, she was barely aware of people passing. Cars driving past slowed to look, and people leaving the café stopped and stared. It took most of the day, with extended breaks for rest and refreshment, but, as she climbed down for the last time and stood back, she sighed with satisfaction.

'That looks good. Even better than I expected. Maybe I will invite Karen to paint the dog in after all.' The haberdashery owner, Brian Millgrove from Balsham, came out to inspect.

'I didn't realise you were starting today. Did the council get their act into gear?' Jill coloured, though her face was already red from the heat of the sun and the day's work outdoors.

'Not exactly yet, but I have had such positive responses I couldn't wait to get started. That is okay, isn't it?'

'Of course, of course. I'm sure there will be less likelihood of graffiti if we have a handsome mural there. Now let me see, who have you got in the picture?'

Jill explained the characters, and Brian sounded a little miffed as he said, 'So I'm not there?'

A sinking feeling in her stomach set in as the potential for people to feel left out dawned on Jill.

'I'm not finished yet, Brian. This is set in the CCCC, at the meeting we had, so I didn't include any of the locals who weren't there. Of course I regard you as a local. But what I have planned is a full sized one of you behind the counter of your shop. I figured it would be better to put that somewhere else. That way people might seek out the shop.'

Brian sounded less than convinced as he grunted, 'That's okay. I'm sure it's not necessary anyway.' And with that he stalked back inside. Jill rolled her eyes and drove home exhausted.

That evening, just when her favourite quiz show had started, her mobile rang, but since it came up as an unknown number, she didn't answer. Much to her annoyance, the ringing was repeated several more times. On the fourth occasion, she answered it, planning to give the person a blast. But that wasn't possible because no one was at the other end. Sighing, she turned the phone off and went to bed.

Stiff and sore the next morning, she wriggled her shoulders to loosen the muscles. 'I wonder if I should give myself a day or two of rest between sessions. I hadn't realised how much reaching and stretching I was doing.' After a hot shower she felt better, had some breakfast, and checked her emails. Much to her surprise, there was one from Laura. They weren't normally on emailing terms. Laura would just arrive at her door or call her. She opened the email.

Dear Jill,

I am writing to tell you that I feel the picture you have drawn of me on the wall of Brian's haberdashery is defamatory. I tried to ring you today but decided this would be better in writing. I would like to formally request that you remove the mural immediately.

Yours sincerely,

Laura

Jill's first instinct was to fire up a defence. She drafted a response.

Dear Laura,

I am sorry you feel my drawing is not up to standard. I have spent hours preparing for this mural, which is intended to show the village of Cowagulac in the light of how friendly and welcoming the villagers are, and how we offer an array of diverse characters. I believe if something is true then it can't be defamatory. Could you explain what you find so objectionable about it?

Regards,
Jill

Shutting her eyes tightly, not pausing to re-read the email, she pressed 'send' and sat back. A reply arrived almost immediately.

You make me look like a fat cow. You aren't so skinny yourself, you know, and I don't think you would like it if someone put a picture of you on a wall looking like that.

Jill checked the photos of the mural that she had taken on her mobile and zoomed in on the outline of Laura. Now she came to look at it, she *had* made Laura much bigger than the other people, and while that was true, it was perhaps a bit hurtful. But then what about Klaus? Ivy? Would they be offended too?

Dear Laura,
I do apologise. I'll paint you out immediately.

She stood to gather her materials, thinking she ought to go sooner rather than later, when the computer pinged again.

Oh, no, I want to be in it, I just don't want to look like a beached whale. Can't you make me smaller?

Jill responded with as much patience as she could muster.

I'll do my best. If you are free, call past this afternoon and we can see how it looks.

Jill rolled her eyes at the computer. 'Honestly, some people are never happy. She wants to be in it, but she doesn't want the artist to show her as she is. So much for my integrity as a painter.'

Next day, the weather was hot again, and Jill collected a large bottle of frozen water to see her through the morning. Her freezer was half full of bottles, as the heat of the day meant the ice didn't last for more than a couple of hours.

Laura was already there when Jill arrived to set up her ladders. Jill groaned internally. She hated having people watching her as she worked. Hopefully she could continue as she had yesterday and lose herself in the project.

There was an awkward moment as the women greeted each other, then Laura gave her a hug. 'I'm sorry I got my knickers in a knot over it. Honestly, it's a fabulous work. I just didn't realise how accurate your painting was, and if that's how people see me, then I'm embarrassed.'

'No Laura, dear, what they see is a charming, efficient, well-meaning organiser who gets things done in a village which needs someone who just gets things done.' And so peaceful relations were *more or less* restored, though Jill did slim down the mural version of Laura until she became half her size. Jill felt comfortable again, and mentally reviewed her other mural plans to make sure no one else would be offended. She felt there was still a slightly strained relationship between them, but surely it would be smoothed over in time. *Ah*, thought Jill, *maybe I could make Laura a beautiful young woman, though still recognizable, maybe buying something in Brian's shop. That would repair the damage for sure.*

There was more feedback from Brian once she had sketched out the next mural, which was on the wall opposite Brian's General Store and Haberdashery. Without needing to look, she could sense that he was hovering constantly, ducking back into his shop to serve the odd customer. With Laura's complaint very much in the forefront of her mind, she chose the most handsome of Brian's features, omitted the scar under his eye, ignored the encroaching grey hair and instead added a twinkle and some laughter lines, as well as a benevolent gesture, as she depicted him handing a little girl a chocolate bar. Brian's reputation was far from one of him being generous, and he was unlikely to have handed over anything free, but a little kindness of spirit might go a long way. In the end, he was delighted with it. 'It looks like a cross between an old-fashioned grocer, with personal service, and a modern supermarket with everything you could want. I'm impressed.' Jill sighed inwardly with relief.

Chapter 9

It was time again.

As Klaus sat in the car watching, waiting, he heard a low hum. He sat up, suddenly wide awake after nearly drifting off, and rubbed his eyes. The hum stayed constant, and Klaus turned his head from side to side, trying to detect the source. Then he saw them. Lights. From high up in front of the car, a piercing green light at first, then it started pulsing. It strobed down to the ground, sweeping in an arc.

'This is not normal. This is it,' Klaus was beyond excited. 'At last, they are here, and I am here to watch them.' His mind raced with thoughts – should he get out of the car and try to attract their attention? Or drive away before they saw him and reversed the light so he was sucked up into the craft? Before he could make a decision, the light faded, and he was left with just the memory.

Chapter 10

The course training day arrived. The plan was for Ingrid to give a short lecture, provide some notes, then the class would sit an open book quiz. Ingrid took her task of running the course very seriously and had devised a program that would be both informative and challenging, albeit not particularly entertaining. Ivy and Geranium had been quick to book in to run their course after the training had been completed. It had been advertised as 'Hidden Memories – back to your childhood.'

As Ingrid waited behind the lectern for the participants, she flipped through the notes she had compiled.

Chapter 1 – Legal Liability and insurance

Chapter 2 – Basic first aid

Chapter 3 – Rights and responsibilities

Chapter 4 – Compiling a course

The last Chapter was not part of the compulsory curriculum as outlined by the political demand, but rather something that Ingrid felt everyone ought to know.

Laura looked surprised when she saw Ingrid had arrived already.

'Oh, hello. I didn't expect you till a bit later.'

Ingrid came down from the stage. 'I wanted to be here bright and early. Did you bring the handouts?'

Laura's eyebrows drew together. 'Naturally. I thought we would put one on each seat, and I'll mark the roll.'

Ingrid nodded appreciation. 'You will be attending too, I hear, even though I understand you are not running a course.'

'Not yet. In the future I will probably run several courses, just to be able to utilise all my experience.'

Ingrid flicked the booklet open. 'I haven't listed all your qualifications in the brochure. Just what are they?'

Laura raised an eyebrow. 'Most of my qualifications are life experience. That, my dear, is not as easily come by as sitting a few exams at a university.'

Their discussion seemed to be heading into acrimonious tones but was cut short by the arrival of a group of participants. Ivy, Geranium, Klaus and Jill arrived at the same time, followed shortly by the rest of the class.

Cups rattled on saucers as people settled into their seats with refreshments.

'Thank you for coming, ladies and gentlemen.' Ingrid's voice permeated every crevice of the old shearing shed, bouncing off the walls and creating feedback, which she promptly corrected by adjusting the speakers.

Ingrid felt unaccustomed nervousness as she stared into the audience, who were rustling their notes, chatting among themselves, and generally looking as though they would prefer to be anywhere else but the CCCC. She knew from village gossip how much everyone was dreading the course.

'If I can refer you to the front page of your handout, you will see the proposed outline of today's course. At the end there will be an open book test.'

Klaus stood up. 'So open book means we can look up the answers if we don't know them?'

'Correct. The instructions we were given covered the content, but the assessment was left up to us, and I don't think the committee felt it was necessary to set an educational style of examination.' A relieved sigh was emitted by the collected attendees.

'I have put the notes onto slides and if you care to watch the screen up here, I will take you through them.'

The course started. Ingrid referred to a number of statutes in her notes, and, as she glanced up from time to time, she could see that some of the members were growing unsettled. There was rustling and low grumbling and raised eyebrows, but no one said anything.

'And in this South Australian case involving a fast-food outlet, a woman successfully sued for the severe burns she received when burnt by a cup containing hot coffee.'

Lionel issued a short bark of laughter. 'What? The only good cup of coffee is a hot cup of coffee, isn't it, Rosie?'

'I would think so. No one would buy a coffee and want it to be lukewarm,' Rosie responded indignantly.

Ingrid continued as though there had not been an interruption. 'The facts of the case, however, were not run of the mill. The woman had purchased the coffee at a drive-through, and, upon obtaining the cup from the attendant, she placed it between her legs. The top of the coffee had not been secured correctly, and it popped off. The resultant spillage of the coffee caused her serious burns.'

'Well of all the …' Laura snorted. 'So now stupidity is being rewarded. What does that mean for us?'

'You might have noticed this.' Ingrid flicked to the next slide, which featured a photo of a takeaway coffee cup with the words printed on the side, *Warning. Contents may be hot.* If refreshment providers do not give warning to their customers about the dangers of their food, however *stupid* we might consider this, then they could be liable.'

'But I don't have that notice up in the café,' Rosie's voice was querulous. 'Do I have to?'

'It's something we will consult with the lawyer about. But we also need to be careful about labelling food items if they have nuts or other allergens in them.'

Klaus glared at Rosie. 'Indeed yes, this most important is. It's a wonder I haven't been seriously ill before this. I shall provide a list of the things I am allergic to, and I would appreciate it if you ensured the ingredients were not in your cooking.'

Lionel fired up in defence of Rosie. 'Blimey, we should just get people to bring their own if it's going to be that difficult. I don't think that's practical, Klaus. No one else has such pernickety dietary needs. And you have managed up till now. In fact, I've seen you wolfing down a vanilla slice when you thought no one was looking.'

Klaus snorted. 'And my stomach paid for it the next day. You could be legally liable if you deliberately try to make me sick, and you will if you don't take care with this.'

'Look, if it gets too difficult then I just won't provide any food,' Rosie said, as though she thought people would deliberately develop a food allergy in order to make trouble. If Rosie withdrew her refreshment services, the town would riot. No one could make a vanilla slice like Rosie. It took considerable time to soothe her fears and for the course to restart.

First aid was covered in a very basic way, and Ingrid requested the committee discuss buying a defibrillator even though the first aid that might be required was most likely going to be the occasional band-aid and headache tablet, though these brought their own issues of allergies and medication clashes.

By the time they got to Rights and Responsibilities, Ingrid decided that she should bring the course to a close and forgo her favourite Chapter, the last one. Maybe she could offer that as an extension course.

Laura led a round of applause for Ingrid as she finished. 'Thank you, Ingrid, most impressive. I suggest we now adjourn for a cup of very hot tea and calorie laden, nut free, gluten free, egg free cakes before coming back for the test.' Relieved laughter followed as they made their way to the kitchen.

Once the hall was empty, Ingrid laid out the test booklets on the chairs, along with a pencil for each person, as she was not sure they would all have their own. Devising the test had been the most difficult part of the program. Ingrid felt it should be challenging but not impossible – she didn't want them to fail. But if the Department wanted to check the program and the assessment, she would have to produce something compelling. Taking a final look around the room she joined the gathering for a cup of tea.

Klaus was bending the ear of Ivy, who cast a look of entreaty at Ingrid. 'Save me,' she mouthed.

In response, Ingrid wended her way over. 'Are you ready for the test, Klaus?' She had failed to interrupt him in full flow of a UFO description. 'And there I was, the light was positively green and flashed across the sky faster than you could see. I know it was my friends leaving, even though I had not seen them arrive. It is most mysterious to me how I can never remember the encounters I have.' Suddenly, he seemed to process that Ingrid had been speaking to him. 'Sorry, what did you say?'

'The test, Klaus, you know, on the stuff I was just teaching you Are you ready for it?'

'Oh that, yes, I'll be fine.' Ivy gave Ingrid a small smile and muttered something about refilling her cup, then slipped away neatly, leaving Ingrid with Klaus.

'Is that tea you are drinking? It's a funny colour.'

'Since you ask,' Klaus peered myopically into the cup, 'it's my very own dried mushroom powder. I have such a surfeit of mushrooms that I am them drying, crushing, then adding some chillies, cinnamon and just a little brown sugar or honey. Pop it all in the blender, and this magnificent powder, full of vitamins, a great hot drink makes. Would you like some?' Ingrid felt vaguely ill at the thought and made an elegant excuse to leave.

Lancelot was talking to Karen in the corner but saw Ingrid approach. 'I must congratulate you, Ingrid. Magnificent p-p-presentation. Almost as good as I could have done, had the c-c-committee asked me. I'm not quite sure why they didn't, but that's life I guess.'

'Thank you, Lancelot.' There was a steely tone in her voice which should have warned Lancelot, but he continued, oblivious. 'In my r-r-role as radio presenter, I come across a lot of lectures, and I have extensive experience in public speaking. If you will forgive me, my dear, I think you could have sped the pace up a little. Though maybe not everyone is as quick as I am at picking up information.'

'Your modesty is to be commended, but I think we should get the assessment over, don't you?' Ingrid turned and clapped her hands.

'Right, everyone, if you have eaten and drunk to your fill, let's get this over with, then we can enjoy the rest of the afternoon doing whatever we wish.'

As they drifted in and took their seats, Laura came up to the microphone.

'Please feel free to start whenever you're ready. Just hand in your booklets when you have finished. And I'd like to thank Ingrid again, for all the work she has put in, and also Rosie for those great refreshments.' A smatter of applause followed, then people started opening their books and writing in answers, some more laboriously than others.

Lancelot was first to stand up and make his way to the front, handing over his booklet and letting out a fulsome sigh. Klaus looked up and frowned. He was struggling, as he only answered every even numbered question, and he wasn't sure whether this would gain him the required pass. No matter how hard he tried, he just couldn't put pencil to paper on those odd numbered questions. *Ironical*, he thought, *Ned would have managed the odd numbers much more easily. But then he probably wouldn't have worried about the evens.* He had reached the last ten questions, multiple choice, thankfully all with four choices, so decided to shut his eyes and guess the answer for the odd numbers. At least that way he had a chance of increasing his result.

Last to finish was Rosie, who had always struggled with literacy. She was sitting next to Laura, who had kindly allowed her to copy most of the answers. This hadn't escaped Ingrid, who chose not to comment. She wasn't sure whether Rosie would have been better off without Laura's help, but that would be shown when she marked them.

Laura packed up the books as the last person left and offered to help Ingrid with the scores.

'Thank you, but I need to have some idea of what parts of the course were a struggle. I might have to present this course elsewhere so it would be handy to know where I can improve.'

Laura nearly asked where on earth she would be required to do this again but bit her tongue before the words escaped. She substituted, 'Very true. Just let me know the results, would you?'

Ingrid was exhausted by the time she got home. A few sips of Baileys and she would start marking. But before the glass was finished, her eyes were closed, and she sank into a sleep of the justifiably exhausted. When she awoke an hour later, bathed in sweat, she felt a slight panic setting in.

How on earth could I have slept? I wonder if I am sickening for something. She fetched a glass of ice-cold water and marked the papers, relieved to find that she could manage to pass all the entrants, although some needed a little help with the eraser and pencil here and there. She called Laura with the good news. 'One hundred percent success rate, Laura. Everyone can teach their courses now.'

'Does that mean we all got a hundred percent? That's most impressive. You were an excellent teacher.'

Ingrid wanted to let this pass over without comment but her innate honesty prevented her from allowing Laura to labour under a misapprehension.

'Not exactly. The highest mark was ninety-eight percent, but some people came very close to not passing.'

Laura gave a small squeak. 'Was it me who got ninety-eight? I thought I did very well, but I'm a bit surprised. I was sure I made a couple of errors.'

There was a pause. 'Actually, it was Lancelot who got that score.'

'Oh. Well, what did I get?'

Laura could hear Ingrid tapping her fingers on the table. 'Well, Laura,' she paused.

'Yes? Come on, it can't be that bad.'

'Actually Laura, I had to sort of make some substitute answers for your paper. It was done in pencil, so I can assure you that no one will know. And I wouldn't have told you if you hadn't pressed me on it.'

'What? You changed my answers? How dare you?'

'I meant it for the best. Otherwise, you wouldn't have passed. I'm sure you knew the right answers, but you were so busy organising everything you probably couldn't concentrate.' She could hear Laura breathing heavily at the other end of the phone.

'I suppose I should thank you, then. I trust you won't tell anyone.'

'Oh, no, of course not. As I said, I'm sure you would normally have done really well.'

'Please send me the list of marks and I will print certificates. Thank you.' And she hung up the phone. Ingrid sat there looking at her mobile for a minute, then shrugged.

'Can't win them all.'

***

When Laura got the list of results, she decided the certificates didn't need to have the score printed on them and instead drew up a 'Statement of Achievement' using the CCCC letterhead and emailed these out. As it happened, there was a meeting of the Cowagulac Local History Group that afternoon, and most of the presenters were there. Laura knew when she walked in that they were all discussing their results as they sipped on the refreshments. Rosie moved among the group, offering shortbreads.

As eager hands reached out to select one, Rosie announced, 'Geranium brought these along, especially for Klaus. They are sugar free, gluten free, and very healthy. A little bit crumbly though.' At the sound of sugar free anything, most hands were withdrawn, and the plate passed quickly to Klaus. He hesitated.

'It is a big adding up thing, such a long word. But it comes to fifty-five, and while that is not divided by two easily, it a double figure is, so I am thinking it acceptable is.' He reached out and took a small biscuit, examining it carefully before popping the whole thing into his mouth. As he continued speaking, small crumbs fell into his beard.

'I'm just glad I passed. Sometimes the grammar a bit confused gets me and I don't know from my right my wrong.' Klaus was quite correct, he did often make errors, but generally people were too kind to point them out.

'Ah, L-l-laura. Thank you for the c-c-c-certificate, but I want to know my s-s-s-score. It's not printed anywhere as f-f-far as I can see.'

Immediately Laura felt in a trap. If she gave Lancelot his score, everyone would want to know what they got. But if she didn't, Lancelot would ask Ingrid whether she had given Laura the results, and Ingrid was far too polite to lie.

'I don't recollect all the scores, Lancelot, but I seem to remember you did well, very well.'

'Not as good as me, I'm sure!' Klaus was cheery in his pleasure at having passed. 'I'm thinking I everything right got.'

Lancelot lifted his eyebrows in a way Laura had learned meant that he was going to pursue things further. 'I think everyone should be g-g-g-given their scores. After all, if we are running c-c-courses we should know our weaknesses.'

By this stage, the discussion had attracted the attention of Ivy, Geranium and Rosie, who all came round clamouring to know the scores. Laura felt under siege, and didn't know what to do.

'Look, I don't have the scores here, but if those of you who want them send me an email, I'll let you know privately.'

'That seems a very good idea, Laura.' Ivy was always supportive and full of common sense. 'Now, let's get our meeting underway. There's such a lot I want to know about the history of this village. As newcomers, Geranium and I just walked in to what most of you have known all your lives. And my specialty is helping people write their life stories, so anyone who wants some guidance on where to begin can let me know.'

Laura breathed a sigh of relief as people took their seats and seemed to forget about the scores. But before the meeting got started, there were two pings from her phone – Lancelot and Klaus both demanding to know their results. Too unsettled to concentrate, Laura didn't stay for the rest of the meeting but went home instead. A large plate of bacon and eggs made her feel more able to cope, and she sent off the scores to those who had asked.

Meanwhile, the meeting had continued without her. Geranium, at the helm in Laura's absence, opened the discussion. 'Could someone summarise the history of Cowagulac for Ivy and myself? We know it's a farming town, settled back in the 1800s. We have already met so many interesting characters.'

The residents looked at each other and no one seemed willing to start. Lancelot glared at Klaus, as though challenging him to take on the role, but finally Lancelot opened his mouth.

'I'm a r-r-relative newcomer here. I moved here about twenty years ago, as a journalist with the l-l-local newspaper. It's only in the last year or two that I have started not to feel like an outsider. After the paper was moved to Balsham, I took over the radio station, and I've been the principal there for close to fifteen years. I take calls from listeners, so I have heard a lot about the problems of the farmers, the mice plagues, about the development that people want or-or-or don't want, and I've overseen the appointment of council and the issuing of grants to some of our outstanding artists such as Ned with his chainsaw art. Truly remarkable, though I must say it's often something I don't quite understand. And, of course, Klaus has been a frequent caller to the radio station, reporting alien visitation. Would you like to continue, Klaus?'

Klaus stroked his beard thoughtfully. 'I have spoken about these creatures before, so there's not much to add. I have seen them, of course, and may have even been abducted. Strange, very strange things have to me happened.' There was some gentle nudging among the audience, and it was quite possible some were thinking about whether Klaus had been refreshing himself with various natural substances before these visits.

Silence fell as Klaus looked around the group. 'My property runs alongside Ned's, and I don't know what's going to happen to that now. I've noticed a bit of coming and going, but there are no for sale signs up. There are a few properties that have been in the same hands for years, but farming is getting more and more financially unrewarding. I don't know what the future holds for us.'

Geranium was taking notes, and now she looked up at Rosie. 'What about you, Aunt Rose? You seem like a fixture in the village.'

Rosie smiled nervously. 'I just run the café. Never had much schooling. In those days you just left when you finished primary school and got a job. My parents ran a café, so I learned the trade when I was a kid, and it seemed natural to take on catering when they died.'

'When was that, Rosie?' Geranium didn't want to upset her, but she knew very little about the bird-like woman.

'I was only seventeen. They both died suddenly, and about a week apart.'

Klaus nodded sagely. 'They were visited.'

Rosie went red in the face and half stood up from her chair. 'Don't you bring that up again. There's no way they were killed by aliens or whatever you think *they* are. They were just worn down and tired from running the business, and there was a bad flu that year.' Klaus rolled his eyes but didn't respond.

Geranium scribbled faster. 'And what about you Jill? What's your story? And Karen?'

Jill looked around the room. 'I don't have a story. I'm just good at art, and this seemed like an arty community. I like it here.'

'And I just like dogs. My sister was here, and it's been nice to have family close.'

Chatter broke out in the group, and Geranium deemed it a good time to call the meeting to an end. She could continue to interview them individually rather than risk everyone becoming restless and allowing tempers to flare.

'Thank you, all, for coming. I'm sure it would be nice if we stayed and had a bit of a social occasion now. I'm happy to talk to anyone who wants to make a time to start on their memoirs.'

Klaus was the first to approach, forming the head of the queue.

'Yes, Klaus?' Geranium's voice was quiet and encouraging, though Klaus generally needed no prompting when it came to talking.

'I'd love people to my life history know. I think it could be very interesting to people, as well as instructive.'

Before long, Klaus and Rosie had signed up, starting the very next week.

Chapter 11

'Come in, dear, and sit down,' Geranium invited Laura into the house. A phone call from Laura after the meeting had inspired Geranium to make Laura the first person to start the memoirs. 'I'm so pleased you could come today. It's an exciting course for Ivy and myself. I'll just start my computer up and open a new folder for you, because this might take a number of sessions.' She turned around for a moment, 'Ivy?' Geranium's voice suddenly went into football barracking volume but was met with silence.

'How annoying. She must be out in the garden again. Sometimes she doesn't put her hearing aids in. Hang on, I'll put the kettle on myself.' Laura had been allocated a session the day after the meeting. Geranium felt that starting with Klaus might leave her too exhausted to do any more than an hour. Between them, the ladies had decided that Geranium would take down the information, and Ivy would tidy it up.

'So much rambling,' Ivy had said when they were discussing the project. 'People don't think in a linear fashion anymore – they go round in circles.'

Left alone, Laura looked around the room. Although the old ladies had only moved in a short time ago, there was no doubt that their personality had been stamped onto this room. Three green, flying ducks made their way up one wall, surrounded by some paintings of unidentifiable country scenes. Laura suspected the frames might be worth more than the artwork itself. Plump cushions were heaped on the couch, and a set of three coffee tables were nesting inside each other, with a crocheted doily on top. A pineapple shaped sugar bowl sat ready for use.

Geranium returned and Laura found herself blushing as though she had been caught prying into Ivy's handbag. Of course she would never consider doing that.

'Ivy was doing some weeding, but she'll bring in the tea when it's ready. Now, shall we make a start? I noticed right at that first meeting you had some interesting things to say about the area. But I want you to tell me about your family first.'

For one of only a few times in her life, Laura felt shy and awkward about talking. But Geranium spoke gently to her, and it wasn't long before the words started to flow. Geranium's fingers flew rapidly over the keyboard, and when Laura commented on this, she said, 'I was brought up on a manual typewriter. This is easy by comparison. Have you ever used a manual typewriter?'

Laura only had a vague idea what it was and shook her head.

'You had to press really hard, and if you made a mistake, there was a little white card to type over the wrong letter. Then you retyped the right letter. It was always better not to make a mistake. But I can also do shorthand – I learned Pitman and was good enough that I could have got a job in court reporting if I wanted. But this isn't my story, we should work on yours. Maybe I could take it down in shorthand and type it up for you later, if the typing is a bit off-putting?'

'No, the typing doesn't bother me. But I don't know where to start, it's confusing.'

'You can begin anywhere, my dear. You've already given me a good five hundred words about your parents. And the good thing about computers is you can just rearrange everything. When I was working, I often had to totally rearrange the order of documents that were sent to me.' Laura wasn't interested in Geranium's working life, so launched off into her history.

'You know that Karen and I grew up near Balsham, with Mum and Dad. We're sisters! Did you have a sister?' Not pausing for an answer, Laura continued, 'Anyway, we didn't get along. If only Karen had listened to me it would have been much better. Mum and Dad always took sides and usually favoured Karen. Dad was a bit of a tyrant, you know, and never let me stay out late or have a boyfriend. Imagine that! Seventeen years old and not allowed out. So, I ran away to Melbourne. There was an odd cousin there and I stayed with her and really saw a different side to life. The things I got up to would make your hair curl. Oh, of course it is curly, sorry. Mum and Dad, especially Mum, wanted me home, and to tell the truth, I didn't like all the people in town. It was too busy, after a small place like Balsham.'

Ivy had brought in the tea, and Geranium paused, hand hovering over the keys. 'What sort of things did you *get up to*?' Laura took a sip of the now cool tea and blushed.

'Well … some things with boys, you know, and some refreshment of the sort that Mum and Dad didn't approve of and which you certainly didn't find in Balsham. But I was soon off all that, didn't like it. It made me feel weird.'

'How long did you stay in Melbourne?'

There was an infinitesimal pause. 'Only about a year. I got a job, but it was just an office thing and a bit boring. I should have finished school, but I wanted to get away.'

'And what about Karen?' Laura's shoulders relaxed at the change of subject, and Geranium realised there was something more that Laura hadn't said.

Laura walked to the window and spoke with her back to Geranium.

'Karen is my only sibling. She took a totally different path to me, what with the dogs and everything. It got a bit much for Mum and Dad, and, eventually, Dad gave her an ultimatum. Either the dogs went, or Karen did. She asked what I thought about her moving to Cowagulac to be with me. And that's how she came to be here. We got on better as we got older. But I'm jumping ahead a bit.'

'Laura my dear, I can't hear you very well when you aren't facing me. Would you mind coming back to the couch?'

When Laura was settled, Geranium noticed her red eyes and recognised the signs of crying. She felt a little guilty but, really, she was too old to be straining her ears to hear what was being said.

'My dear, I get the feeling that there's something you haven't mentioned. It's just you and me here.' Right on cue, a crashing and banging sound started in the kitchen as Ivy began to clean up. Geranium added, 'And Ivy, but,' she went on, 'none of this needs to go into your biography if you don't want it to.'

The tears started flowing again and then a violent sobbing stopped any conversation. Geranium fetched a glass of water and sat beside Laura.

'There, there my dear. I'm no psychologist, but I wonder if talking about whatever it is will help.'

Slowly the hiccups subsided, and Laura nodded. Hesitating, she stuttered a little before starting the story.

'He – or she – would be in their teens now. I try not to think about it, but it comes back every night. I shouldn't have done it. If my parents knew …' she trailed off.

'We are talking about a baby, are we? And a termination?' Geranium couldn't think of any other cause of such distress. 'I take it this was when you were in your wild youth down in Melbourne?'

Laura snuffled and blew her nose with determination. 'Yep. I don't even know who the father was. It was one of those parties where there were drugs and alcohol, and I thought I was so grown up and mature and I don't really know what happened. Maybe I was drugged or date raped or something. Anyway, I ended up pregnant. Of course, I couldn't tell Mum and Dad, so my cousin arranged for an abortion. It was awful. I was so sick afterwards. That's really why I left Melbourne and moved here, where no one knew me. But I found out that this town is so bigoted, if they knew what I had done I would be ostracised. And I don't want that to happen because I have found a real life here.'

'Does Karen know? About the abortion?' Laura shuddered at the word but nodded. 'She found out one day when she called around and I was crying. It would have been the kid's first or second birthday, I forget which. I couldn't think of anything to tell her except the truth.'

'How did she take it?'

Laura paused and gave this some thought. 'Usually, Karen is pretty easy going. She just has the dogs and gives them all her love. We have a sort of love-hate relationship – I think she is jealous of me and all I have built up here, and she was always under the thumb of our dad.'

Geranium sighed. 'I can imagine it was a distressing time for you. You've done so well to be in charge of organising so much here in town.'

Laura gave a watery chuckle. 'That's very kind of you, but I think Lance is a better organiser than me, though don't tell him I said that. People here are more interested in their farms and families than in the things I have tried to organise. It's been disheartening.'

Ivy came in and smiled at Laura as she mimed a question about whether more tea was required. Laura shook her head. Ivy cleared the teacups and tiptoed out.

'What sort of things have you done here? I think they should all be described in your biography. Let's make a list and then we can expand on it later.'

Laura wrinkled her brow as she tried to recall the things she had attempted. 'Oh, yes, there was a dance club. I thought the women of Cowagulac should get out a bit, since they often worked on the farms during the day. But that was the trouble – only women came! The married ones didn't want to dance with other women and the single ones came looking for a man. So that only lasted a few weeks.'

Ivy called out from the kitchen. 'I'd go to a dance club if there were men. But they would have to be rich and single!' Geranium got up and closed the door to the kitchen, rolling her eyes at Laura.

Laura giggled. 'That sort of man is pretty thin on the ground, I'd have to say. Especially here. Anyway, after that I started a photo and camera club. There were quite a few men there, but they only took photos of rutting bulls or cow udders. You've no idea how many variations on the sex act of cows are possible to capture.' She glanced up, to see Geranium had opened her eyes wide and was frowning. 'Oh, I'm sorry, I didn't mean to embarrass you.'

'No, my dear, no problems. I was just imagining … probably best not to do that! What happened to that club?'

'I offered some prizes from the regional paper. I think the editor imagined sunset over Mermaid Mountain, or a day in the life of a rural family, and instead the only entries were too embarrassing to submit. I had to forfeit the prizes and say the farmers were all too busy to enter the competition.'

Ivy, who had returned to clear the plates, was standing at the now open door, covering her mouth as she stifled a laugh before heading back into the kitchen, and even Geranium had a twinkle in her eye.

'Oh dear. I see your dilemma. Was there anything else?'

Laura reddened slightly. 'Just one other. I advertised a debating society and booked the municipal office. No one came. I just sat there for an hour, then locked up and went home. That's why I was so glad when the CCCC came along. And I asked Karen to move here too, and it's been the best thing I ever did.'

Geranium was pleased that Laura seemed to have recovered from the disclosure about the abortion, but she had a few more questions.

'Laura, how did you come to choose Cowagulac? For Ivy and me, we just closed our eyes and jabbed a pin in a map, and we're so happy with the outcome. I have often wondered what our lives might have been like in any other country town. But what about you?'

'It was quite an easy choice for me. Mum and Dad live near Balsham, so I was aware of the town, and there was a house here that suited me, so off I went. After they died, of course I could have moved back, but there were too many memories.'

Geranium nodded sagely, then pushed her chair back from the computer, and went to sit on the couch next to Laura. Taking her hand, she patted it gently.

'There is one other thing I wanted to ask, my dear. You don't have to answer it, and I don't want to upset you, but it's about the … city problem you mentioned. Is that all right?'

'As long as you don't mind me crying again.'

'Thank you. You said you don't know who the father was. Are you sure you have no idea?'

There was a long pause. 'All right, I do know who it was. But I've never seen him again and I don't want to.'

'Did he know you were pregnant? And were having an abortion?'

Laura bit her lips. 'Yes, and yes. But I'm not answering any more questions.'

'I understand. We have a lot to go on with. Let's meet again next week.'

After the door had closed behind Laura, Ivy walked into the living room and met Geranium's eye. 'Well, what about that?' Ivy mused. She was always the more curious of the two, Geranium the more accepting.

'It's really none of our business,' Geranium chided. 'I'm just writing the biography. I think we should forget she ever told us anything.'

Chapter 12

Emerging refreshed from the bathroom, Karen came face to face with her sister, standing in the middle of the lounge room. 'Oh! I thought you were a burglar!' Laura frequently came in and out of the house without standing on ceremony.

'For once the dogs didn't bark. I think they might be getting used to me. About time, after, what, three years?'

Karen put the kettle on. 'Dumpling is four, Colleen is three, and the others are all under two. I'm glad to have got Colleen off to the dog sitter while she bonds with the puppies. Much as I adore them, I couldn't manage all these adult dogs as well as a nursing mother. And I have my class to prepare for. Did you know there are twelve people booked in?'

Laura's nose wrinkled. 'Yes, I think you did mention it, just once or twice. Maybe three times. What do you plan to do in the class?' Laura ripped open a packet of chocolate biscuits using her teeth and crammed one into her mouth.

'I'll take canvases, paper, pencils, charcoals, and my oils. I won't let the class use my oil paints, though. I thought I'd get them to start sketching on paper, then doing a charcoal version, before those who want to do the advanced class can buy their own oils. In the meantime, I can continue with my own painting for the art show. I've run off some posters and I'll put them up at the Baringabye Dog Show this weekend. I might have a full class, that would bring in a bit of cash. Are you coming with me to the dog show?'

Karen poured the boiling water onto tea leaves in the pot, then swirled the water around before pouring out two cups.

Laura started on her third biscuit. 'Sure. How many dogs are you taking?'

'Just Whisky Darling and maybe Ringo. Ringo isn't quite ready for showing yet, but I've entered Whisky in the two-year-old category. We would have to leave by about seven though. Is that too early?'

The sisters made plans. Karen drank two cups of tea, having raised a thirst, but Laura barely touched her cup, preferring instead to motor through another two chocolate biscuits. Karen threw her a glance but knew better than to comment. She had noticed the weight Laura had stacked on recently, but history indicated that this was part of a yo-yo cycle, whereas Karen was blessed with a stork-like figure no matter what she ate. But, because of the dogs, she did much more exercise than Laura ever did.

The final plan was that Laura would bring her four-wheel drive over, which had room for two large crates to be put in the back, as Laura didn't want dog hair everywhere in the car. Karen conceded that it was difficult taking passengers in her car because the dogs expected to sit in the front seat.

The weather stayed hot and dry, so it was a pleasure for Karen to sit back in cooled comfort and let her sister drive.

When she drove her own car there was no point in operating the aircon, as the dogs needed the windows half open, and Karen had no intention of trying to air-condition the outdoors.

Conversation was desultory during the drive. Karen thought about discussing the issue of diets but didn't want any unpleasantness. Neither sister commented to the other about their contrasting shapes, though the seat belt was stretched rather tight around Laura's body. They had experienced a few ups and downs in their sisterly lives, with arguments about men, dogs, and spending inheritances. Karen sank most of hers into the dogs, where Laura saved and invested, and told Karen in no uncertain words that it was a silly decision to get rid of her entire portion of the estate into unproven animals. So, given past experience, they both kept the chatter light-hearted and general for the duration of the drive. As they pulled into a space marked *Competitors Only*, Karen suddenly shivered. 'Someone must have walked over my grave,' she murmured under her breath.

The sisters separated, Karen setting up in the competitors' tent while Laura put up some posters, then strolled around the stalls and watched some of the obedience trials. She was especially fascinated by an exhibition of flyball, barracking enthusiastically as large and small dogs ran a course involving jumping barriers, running through a tunnel and eventually getting to a tennis ball at the end which they were meant to pick up and return to their owners. Some were excellent, others so distracted that they just ran straight to their handler without even attempting the course. Some were brave, tackling jumps that seemed far too big for them, while some of the larger dogs stood and looked in a puzzled manner at the tunnel before either walking away disdainfully or running enthusiastically and emerging somewhat surprised at the other end. Laura found the time passed quite happily, and after buying a salad roll, large muffin and pleasantly hot latte at the café – checking first to make sure there was a heat warning on the cup – she went to meet Karen.

'Look, second prize to Whisky! It's the first time we have entered a show, so perhaps he will be a prize dog in a year or two, then his sperm will be worth a lot more.' Laura was delighted for her sister, and they drove home in the setting sun, in a good mood with the world and each other. Laura did idly wonder how one milked sperm from a dog and had a few visions of Karen chasing him round the kitchen with a test tube, but she just smiled to herself and didn't ask Karen how it was done.

Chapter 13

Geranium arranged for Klaus to have his first session the day after Laura's. She opened a new file on the computer and sat poised ready to translate Klaus's rough and ready English into proper writing. She had spread a towel across the couch before he arrived, as she had noticed several times that his clothing lacked a certain cleanliness, depending on whether he had been gardening, collecting honey, or sitting out in the moonlight. However, when he arrived, it was evident he was had spruced himself up, and he explained that this was a momentous occasion for him. 'Never have people an interest in me taken. I am flattering.' Geranium smiled and didn't bother to correct him.

'Well, you're an interesting man. Just begin where you want to Klaus, and we can rearrange things later.'

He settled on the couch and sipped a concoction of dried mushroom tea, which he had brought with him. 'The stomach ache I have had for the day past,' he said. 'Very uncomfortable. Many trips to the toilet. Hoping that now all finished is.'

'What a pity. So annoying when one must stay close to a bathroom.' Geranium always used the more polite terminology for bodily functions. 'I do hope you have recovered. When you are ready, just begin.' Klaus squared his shoulders as he prepared to launch into his history. Ivy sat in one corner of the room, quietly knitting. Klaus put down his cup and began.

'You will be with my English impressed, for sure. My native language German, of course is, and I to this country came when I was very little. My parents were given some money by the government here to come and help populate the small country towns, so I have grown up in country very like Cowagulac. It was not easy for me at school. The other children treated me as though we were still in the middle of the war and every German was a possible traitor, so I often didn't go to school, though of course my parents didn't know this until the teacher wrote reports. For me it was more interesting roaming the countryside than sitting in a classroom.'

Geranium narrowed her eyes and looked at Klaus. 'And yet I imagine school was not difficult for you?'

'Anything with numbers easy came to me, but words were a different matter. This English to learn is difficult. What sort of language has words like *wind* and *wind* which are the same letters but mean different things? German is much more sensible.'

'I don't know much German, Klaus, but I have seen writing in German where the whole line is just one word. That's not easy.'

'Ach!' Klaus uttered a frustrated German exclamation. 'You write my story, and I teach you German. No time at all until you can look at one of those long words and understand.'

Geranium looked pointedly down at the computer. 'We'd better keep going, I think. Your life will cover many interesting topics, I'm sure.'

Klaus settled back and rubbed his temples with two pointy forefingers. 'Where was I? Ah, yes. I got to know the shearers who came every year, and they taught me to shear the sheepses. You can see I am still a big, strong man, though with age I am more stooped and certainly could not do six sheep every hour. I don't think I could even turn one over on its back anymore. After a while, when I got good at the task, they just took me with them, traipsing from farm to farm. I must have been about fourteen, and my parents had given up on getting me to school. I think there was an inspector who paid them a visit once, and wanted to know where I was, but I don't think they got into trouble.'

'Your parents are no longer with us?' Ivy spoke for the first time, and Klaus looked around as though he had forgotten she was there.

'They died many years ago. I saw them once a year when the shearers to my home town returned. They wanted me to come home but it was a good life, out in the open. I had nothing to come home to. We ate well, slept well, and not talking much. Gradually my English slipped away, and I talked to the sheepses in German. I think they liked it. The other blokes ended up calling me the sheep whisperer. 'Guten Tag, meine kleine Lämmchen,' I bent low and spoke in their ear, and though they twitched and baaed, they settled and let me cut their wool with long, firm strokes.'

Klaus had a faraway look in his eyes, and Geranium imagined he was mentally back in the harsh Australian outback, physically exhausted from the demanding work of shearing. Klaus gave a little shake and continued.

'After we finished one farm we moved on to the next, and so I learned about the geography of Victoria. We often slept under the stars, and that is how I came to see my first UFO.' Klaus's eyes sparkled and he walked to the window and stared out, perhaps in case a UFO was lurking.

'Naturally, I didn't mention it to any of the others – I think you can imagine that the bullying I got at school would be magnified a trillion times if I was bullied by the shearers.' Klaus glared at Geranium from under his bushy eyebrows, as though challenging her to dispute his statement. Geranium merely nodded and looked up encouragingly. 'They were tough men who drank their pay the day it was given to them. I saved mine and put it in the bank. I started to sleep further out from the group, and over time they seemed to accept that I preferred to be alone. I started to experiment with native foods, and it seemed a logical thing to a vegetarian become.'

Hands hovering over the computer, Geranium enquired, 'Do you want to talk any more about your first alien visitation?'

Klaus leaned forward and put his now-cold cup of mushroom tea on the table with a bang that made Ivy wince.

'I saw the lights.' Klaus spoke so softly that Geranium strained to hear him. 'I was out on my own, with just the sheepses, when their stirring and baaing woke me up. One sheepses nudged me with her nose, as though wanting me to look up. And I did. And lights in the sky there were. But even as I looked at them, the lights disappeared. Then they came back, closer, brighter, faster. The sheepses were a racquet making and I see torch light from other shearers. When I back look, the lights are gone.' He fell silent.

'That is a most interesting story, Klaus. However, I'm afraid we must finish here for the session, but we can meet again next week.'

'Then I can you tell about how I found the numerology was the most important structure in my life. We must meet on the second, fourth, or sixth. That good will be. And I can tell you about being abducted—'

'I can't wait,' Geranium jumped in before Klaus could get carried away with his story. 'Thank you for telling me so much. I will polish my notes and email them to you.' Geranium shepherded Klaus to the door and rolled her eyes as she shut it firmly behind him.

Chapter 14

Although the weather was cooler now that April had arrived, it was still humid. Jill showered and put on her bra and knickers before preparing breakfast. Gazing out the window while she waited for the kettle to boil, she held a one-sided conversation with a magpie, which had fixed her with a steely eye, indicating a desire for a meaty breakfast. 'I wonder what you would be like as a person,' mused Jill. 'Let me see … demanding. Neat, and very tidy. Charming in your own way – when you want something. Hmmm, you sound a bit like my ex.'

Teacup in hand, Jill returned to the lounge room. Catching a sudden movement, she almost spilt the hot tea over her feet.

'Oh! My goodness, Laura, you gave me such a fright. I didn't hear you come in.' She put the cup down and hastily picked up the washing from the basket she had brought in and covered the front of her underwear-clad body. 'Honestly, I was so startled. I was in my own world. I'm sorry Laura. Just let me get dressed. Would you like a cuppa?'

Laura handed her a dress from the floor. 'My fault entirely. I did call out, but no one answered, and the door was open.' She moved towards the kitchen. 'Don't worry about me, I can make a coffee myself. It's not the first time I've been in your kitchen, you know.'

Jill was sweating and still a little unsteady on her feet. She had really got a fright, thinking she was totally alone in her house. Goodness, she was nearly naked! What short of shock would have that been for Laura? Bad enough that her voluminous panties and bra were on display.

Once Jill was dressed, they chatted amicably about the training session and the test. 'I was so insulted, though, when Ingrid said I had nearly failed. I mean, I thought those questions were dead easy. What did you get, Jill?'

'I don't remember. I do have a bit of a short-term memory problem, and if something isn't important it just disappears out of my brain.'

As time went on, Jill started wondering if Laura was ever going to leave. She smothered a yawn and girded her nerves to say something to give Laura a hint.

Then she had a brainwave. In her sewing experience, people rarely wanted to help. She still had a lot of clearing up to do after the costumes she had made for the launch because she had moved straight on to painting the mural. There was a large tangle of sequinned trims which she had used for the parrot wings, but the colours were all entwined, and it was tricky to disentangle them without the sequins falling off. That would be a perfect task – either Laura would do it, and then the boring task would be done, or she would invent an excuse and leave. Either solution would work.

She looked at Laura. 'I'm wondering if I could ask a favour?' The narrowing of her eyes told Jill that Laura was a little suspicious about the sort of favour that might be asked.

'Of course,' she said without enthusiasm, 'ask away.'

Jill leaned into the large cardboard box at her side and pulled out the skein of trims. 'I wondered if you would have a go at untangling these for me?'

'Of course. What should I do with the different colours?' Laura had already started tugging at the skein, making the knots tighter.

'Here, let me show you how to do it. Sometimes you will get to a knot that you can't undo, and in that case, cut it, but generally the longer the stretch of trim, the easier it is to attach it to a costume.' Jill showed Laura how to tease out the ends, untangle the sequins and lay the strands out on the table. 'Just do as much as you feel like. I shan't need the trim for a while, so there's no hurry. I'll just pop the kettle on again.'

In the space of time it took for Jill to fill the kettle, Laura discovered that the task allotted to her was not to her taste. The sequins were sharp and tiny, and the threads binding them impossible to break. She was formulating an excuse to leave when Jill's head reappeared round the door.

'Milk and one? Won't be a tick.' Laura opened her mouth to begin her excuses, but Jill had disappeared. Standing, Laura picked up the mess of shiny discs from her lap and dumped it back in the box. Several strands of errant sequins adhered to her clothes, and Laura picked up the scissors to cut them free. Just as she did so, Jill brought in the tea, two mugs in one hand and a plate of half melted Tim Tams in the other.

'I'm sure you aren't hungry, but I always think there's room for a little biscuit, don't you?' Jill headed towards the small table, but it was already covered with sequins. At the same moment, Laura stepped forward to help her, tripped on the trailing strands and fell forward. As though in slow motion, Laura saw the two mugs flying to the floor, tea propelled in all directions, biscuits falling with a wilted thud on the floor. Thrusting her hands out to save herself from being burnt by the tea, Laura's grip on the scissors didn't waver, and the blades pierced Jill's neck. Jill collapsed to the floor with a shriek, followed by a gurgle.

Not believing her eyes, Laura momentarily took in the scene before she screamed at Jill's comatose body, finally dropping the bloodied scissors to the ground with a resonant clang.

Outside Jill's house, Rosie had stopped to listen to the musical tune of the magpie and was speaking to the bird when she heard the commotion. At first, she thought it was the radio, but when the bird tossed its head in the direction of the front door, Rosie took a decisive step.

'Something's wrong, you say? Should I go in?' The magpie flew to the doorstep and nodded its head again. Hesitating no longer, Rosie opened the screen door and was met with what looked like a massacre. Blood had gushed from the wound in Jill's neck, mingling with the brown tea and lumps of biscuit which had disintegrated on the floor. Here and there among the congealing blood was the occasional bright gold or red sequin, adding a festive, Christmassy touch to the scene. Laura was standing over the body, the volume of her screaming ever-increasing. As Rosie took in the scene,

Laura's scream reached a climax, and she promptly vomited over Jill.

Rosie's eyes opened wide. She had no idea what to say, making her silence a truly memorable instance.

'Help, Rosie, get an ambulance!' Laura wiped her mouth with her bloodstained hand.

'What …? Who …? My God, what happened?' Rosie stood unmoving, as though her feet were glued to the ground.

'Rosie! Snap out of it and ring for help! Have you got your mobile?' Laura was rapidly regaining command of her senses. 'Here, give it to me.' She snatched the phone from where she could see it sticking it out of Rosie's pocket. 'See if you can help Jill. Quickly now.'

Now that someone was able to give her direction, Rosie regained her sense of purpose and knelt by Jill, hesitatingly putting a finger to her neck. 'I can't feel a pulse. I don't think she's breathing.' But Laura wasn't listening, she was already speaking to emergency services.

'Yes, at Jill's house, you know Jill. It's the second last one on Wombat Drive, with the petunias out the front. Please hurry.'

Laura pushed Rosie out of the way and rolled Jill onto her back. Her memory of CPR training came to the fore, though it was some years since she had refreshed her skills. Anxious to be able to restart Jill's heart, she pulled the scissors out of the wound in Jill's neck.

A spurt of blood hit Laura in the face as the scissors ceased to plug the wound, and Laura fell back as though she had been shot. Spitting blood out over the carpet, she wiped her mouth with her t-shirt and leaned over Jill, positioning her hands over her sternum and started compressions. But the blood kept coming, though the stream was weakening, which made Laura think that Jill must be running out of blood. Rosie ran back in, and exclaimed 'No, Laura, we must stop the bleeding first. Where's a towel?' She frantically ran through the house, gathering towels from the bathroom and kitchen, and throwing them at Laura. Laura used the first to wipe the blood from her arms, but Rosie ran over and pushed her aside.

'Here, we need to stop Jill bleeding, not you. Go and wait for the ambulance.' Laura got to her feet and wandered outside in a daze, while Rosie staunched the blood and packed the wound with towels.

'Jill, Jill, I'm here, stay with me Jill, you'll be okay.' There was an ominous lack of movement from Jill, and no response. The sound of sirens in the distance caused Rosie to stop and sit back on her heels, wiping her brow and breathing a silent prayer of thanks.

The ambulance officers took over and dealt quietly and effectively with the situation, attaching tubes and oxygen canisters and masks to the inert body, then rolling Jill onto a stretcher and screaming off along the road towards the hospital. Rosie sat exhausted in the only chair that was unstained by blood and stared out the window. Laura was nowhere to be seen, but, within a few minutes, a police car pulled up and Constable Makepeace emerged, his long-limbed body uncoiling from the driver's seat. He stopped and took out his notebook before wiping his feet carefully on the mat and entering.

'I'm so glad to see you, Constable,' said Rosie, not moving from the chair. 'What a disaster.'

The policeman just stood and looked at the room, then the colour drained from his face, and he made a hasty exit to the front garden where Rosie could hear him vomiting copiously into the hydrangeas.

Hmm, thought Rosie, looking around, *I suppose it was a bit of a shock. I don't expect the poor chap has been faced with anything like this before.* Her standard answer to any event was a cup of tea, so she went to the kitchen.

Constable Makepeace appeared at the back door, looking rather sheepish. 'Sorry about that, Rosie. I wasn't expecting such a scene. I've shut the front door and called for the sarge. This isn't something I can do by myself.' Rosie made an unspoken query, gesturing to the kettle. 'Yes, I'd love a cup. Lots of sugar please.'

They sat in companionable silence at the kitchen table.

'She's dead, isn't she?' Rosie's tone of voice was resigned.

'Afraid so. Pronounced dead on the way to the hospital. Loss of blood. Do you know what happened?'

'I only arrived afterwards. Laura was here, though. I don't know where she's gone to.' Rosie looked around as though expecting Laura to emerge from a cupboard or under the table. 'I expect she could fill in some of the gaps.

But when I got here, Jill was already on the floor and Laura was standing over her.'

'Maybe you'd better wait and let me write this all down in a statement.' As he spoke, another police car rolled to a stop by the back door.

'Thank goodness, that's the sarge. He can take over.'

After some instruction from the sergeant, Rosie and Makepeace headed back to the police station so Rosie could make her statement.

There was still no sign of Laura.

Chapter 15

As the final chords of 'Three Little Maids' screeched to its conclusion, Lancelot cleared his throat and hummed silently under his breath. A singing teacher had once told him that making a siren sound in his throat warmed up the vocal cords, and it was a technique he had followed religiously ever since. He wasn't sure it made any difference, and certainly had no effect on his stammer, but he felt better for doing it.

The time pips started, Lancelot slid the volume lever up on the mixer, and picked up the top sheet of paper from the pile that Rosie had slid onto his desk, right next to the microphone.

'Good a-a-a-afternoon, this is Lancelot Charger, bringing you the news in brief on this sunny afternoon in Cowagulac, Maniagallup, Baringabye, and surrounds. Firstly, the weather. Hot. Maximum of thirty-two degrees and no sign of rain. There's a sheep heat weather alert for lambs. And now the h-h-h-headlines.

Police were called to the home of a local woman this morning, after an emergency call to ambulance and police s-s-services. A body was found, and an injured local woman was located nearby. She was taken to hospital.' Lancelot pressed the 'cough' button which momentarily took him off air. 'Good God!'

He released the button, but was shaken, and had to speak more slowly to regain control of his voice. 'Police expect to release a further statement later this afternoon.' He wiped a drop of sweat from the desk where it had fallen and continued. 'Several c-c-cows disappeared overnight from a field in Redgrave, north of Maniagallup. The cows were ear-tagged, and police hope to be able to lay charges shortly.'

He stopped for a breath. 'Balsham Music Store reports that Velvet Starshine's new single is making waves among the music community, and stock is selling fast. Velvet recently released 'I do not believe in the possibility of an interventionist deity, but,' and hopes to make this her first step on the ladder of commercial music success. And, ladies and gentlemen, we will be interviewing Velvet herself soon, so stand by for more details in coming days. Now, some music.'

Still sweating with the shock of the news he had just read, Lancelot threw on the nearest CD which happened to be Handel's *Hallelujah Chorus* and mopped his brow. The glorious strains of the music soothed him, and he leaned back in the chair and patched the mike through to Rosie, who he could see through the soundproof window.

'Rosie, what's this about a local woman? Did you know about it?'

'It's Jill Taylor. I can't say any more than that.'

Lancelot sat back in his chair. 'Why didn't you tell me? This is awful. I only saw her yesterday and she was as fit as a fiddle.'

Rosie blushed and looked down, but answered the phone the moment it started to ring. Lancelot had to return to the turntable and set up the next recording, so it wasn't until an hour later, as his program drew to a close, that he was able to talk with Rosie.

'And that's the end of my p-p-program for today. Bill Suttie is waiting to take over for 'Animal Hour'. Thank you for listening, and till next time, this is Lancelot C-charger signing off.' He pressed the button to transfer control to Bill, who gave him a thumbs up.

In the control room, Lancelot sat on the desk and looked down sternly at Rosie. 'What's it all about? I've known you for too long Rosie, you can't fool me. What happened?'

The tiny, bird-like lady looked away. 'I was near Jill's place. I heard Laura scream. I went in, called the ambulance, and that's really all I know. Honestly, Lance, you'll need to ask the police if you want to know any more. I've given them a statement and they told me not to talk to anyone. I'm very shaken. Very. I nearly didn't come in, but I know how hopeless you are managing by yourself.' She gathered her bag and straw hat and headed for the door. Lancelot watched her go, calling out, 'Thanks for coming in,' but under his breath adding, 'Thanks for nothing.' He shook his head.

He was puzzled by what was missing from Rosie's meagre account of the drama. Who was the mysterious woman who had been taken to hospital? Obviously not Jill, if she was dead. How had the accident happened? Was it a crime? Why hadn't he heard anything more? He called the hospital, but they wouldn't give out any information. 'Bloody privacy laws,' he exclaimed as he hit the 'end call' button with a vicious jab. 'I'm a journalist, and what help do I get? None.' He searched his contact list for anyone else who might know something.

Karen Adams! She had her finger pretty much on the pulse and was much more approachable than her stuck-up sister, Laura. Anyone who liked dogs as much as Karen had to be a good egg. He pressed the dial button, then walked around the office waiting for an answer, having set the phone on loudspeaker. Lancelot had a strong disdain for being kept waiting and having nothing to do. He blamed it on his self-diagnosed attention deficit hyperactivity disorder.

Finally, a breathless voice answered the phone. 'Yes?' it said impatiently. 'Who is it?'

'L-lancelot here, Karen. I just read the news headlines on my program. That's terrible news about Jill.'

'I'm too busy to talk at the moment, Lancelot. I've got Laura in hospital, the dogs to feed, and I'm organising my dog portrait class for the community centre. I have a full class booked in already, and I'm meant to be at the dog show today to pick up supplies. What do you want?'

Lancelot was a little taken aback. He thought he and Karen had a good relationship, but she was really cutting him short. However, he now knew who the local woman who had been taken to hospital was. It was Laura.

'I'm sorry to hear Laura isn't well. Anything I can do to help?'

Her voice was softer. 'Thanks Lance, but there's nothing. She's being well looked after; it was just the shock. She had a bit of a panic attack, and she got a bad cut on her hand. I don't think she'll be in for more than another day, it's just the timing is shocking. And of course, she feels terribly guilty about Jill.'

'Of course.' Lancelot was frantically trying to add two and two so that he could work out what Laura had to do with Jill's death, but he couldn't reveal his lack of knowledge to Karen. 'Shocking, and so unexpected. But I shouldn't hold you up, you have heaps to do.' He secretly hoped this would prompt Karen to stay on the line now that he had stopped pushing for details and was a little surprised when it did.

'No Lance, not at all, I appreciate you calling. I'm mostly organised, it's just you know, hospital visits are always stressful, and the police have been hovering around Laura's bed and won't let anyone talk to her. Our family has never had to deal with the police before.'

'Do you want me to talk to my solicitor? We have a great guy for the radio station's legal issues, and I know him well.'

Karen's voice became a little stiffer and Lancelot winced when he heard it. 'No, thank you, Lancelot. Laura has done nothing wrong, absolutely nothing, and we have no need for legal help. Now I must go.' And with that the call was severed.

Lancelot sat firmly in the swivel chair in the reception area and rocked back and forth. Something smelled fishy. He wasn't an investigative journalist for nothing. And here, on his own home turf, things were going more than a little bit wrong. First Ned, now Jill, violently and unexpectedly dead.

Lancelot had tried to teach Constable Makepeace in a Bible study class when the officer was young, and he wasn't particularly impressed with his intelligence. 'I wonder if I could do something through my radio program. Maybe I can put out some feelers, do some interviews. That's certainly something to think about.'

Lancelot headed home and opened the computer. He was a dab hand at Excel spreadsheets, but he struggled to work out what headings to use in his new project. *Suspects?* But these might have been natural – if unfortunate – deaths. *Cause of death?* That was clear enough for Ned, at least. *Enemies?* There was an open field there – Ned was not popular in many quarters, though Jill never seemed to offend anyone. He needed a dossier of the evidence, and it had to be accurate and complete. But it was so hard to get all the information he needed. The police weren't interested in the sudden deaths except in so far as autopsies being needed, and this put pressure on Balsham, which had the only the medical facilities. As far as Lancelot could tell, it didn't seem at all odd to anyone else that two people had died – it just seemed like the norm to them, but really, at this rate, half of Cowagulac would be shuffled off, and a potential murderer allowed to run free. Goodness, he might even be next! Surely these were accidents. But what if they weren't?

The thought was so shocking that he immediately set to work completing the spreadsheet.

First, he should list the people who had died or disappeared in the preceding few months. If he listed *everyone* that would include old Mrs Raelene McGill from the nursing home, who was ninety-two after all, Stu 'Stupot' Taggers who ran himself over with his own tractor, and the mysterious departure of Crystal Brook from the town, after an ill-conceived affair with the dentist. Strictly speaking, it was assumed she was still alive but hiding out somewhere in the big smoke. With these three deaths – or potential deaths – in mind, he decided to stick to the suspicious deaths: those of Ned and Jill.

Ned had his jugular severed by his own chainsaw. How likely was he to lose control of an instrument he had used for years? On the one hand, not at all likely, as he was very familiar with the saw, and made confident cuts into large tree stumps. On the other hand, he did fiddle with his machinery to make it more adapted to his needs. He was known to be quite eccentric, and did have problems with emotional control – Lancelot remembered his outburst at the planning meeting, as well as his brusque reaction when invited to appear on the radio show. 'Not bloody likely,' were the exact words. And he had nearly thumped that wretched politician when he came to their meeting. There were no witnesses to Ned's death except Laura, and, according to local gossip, Laura had the hots for Ned and wouldn't be likely to kill him off.

He had learned that Jill was stabbed in the neck in a most unfortunate way. Brand-new, razor-sharp scissors, tripping on loose fabric. But, once again, the only witness was Laura. Rosie arrived on the scene soon after, but it didn't seem like she was talking. He knew Laura had given the scissors to Jill as a thank you gift, but as to how the incident happened, that was a mystery.

Of the two, Ned was the least liked, but Lancelot didn't think he was hated by anyone. Except maybe Klaus, as they had constant arguments about the greenie imperative and Klaus was always whinging about Ned's noisy machinery. But then, Klaus believed in aliens, so that was enough to put him in the 'loony' category. He thought back to one of Klaus's stories – the one where he claimed that one night, about six months ago, he was sucked up from his car and deposited back in the morning about fifty metres away from here he had started. He recalled Klaus looking quite shaken and white-faced when he talked about it, but everyone thought Klaus had just had a few too many nips of whisky before going out to wait for his extra-terrestrial visitors.

Suddenly, Lancelot recalled a newspaper report about a tourist seeing a thylacine cross the road in front of her when she was driving along Mermaid Gully Road. 'Everyone knows they are extinct. Stupid woman.' But there it was, large as life, in the local rag. *Tasmanian Tiger Lives* was the front-page headline. The interview, he recalled, was lightweight at best. The woman was a city slicker, no experience in the bush, wouldn't know a mangy fox from a goat, in his opinion. Maybe he should get this woman together with Klaus. 'They'd make a fine pair,' he chuckled to himself, though when he recalled there was a violent death at hand, he felt guilty and hastily shut his spreadsheet down.

Meanwhile, Makepeace was finally allowed into the hospital to interview Laura. Her arm was bandaged, her face was white, and she was dressed in a crisp hospital gown. A plastic bag with her bloodstained clothes was on the chair beside her.

'This isn't too good, Laura. Do you feel up to giving me a statement? And thank you for keeping those clothes for me – the sarge said they might need to be sent for forensics. Don't know why, really, it's only going to be your blood or Jill's.' He shuddered as he remembered the scene, and Laura's bottom lip quivered. Makepeace sat on the chair next to the bed and opened his notebook.

'Do I have to talk about it?' Laura's voice was weak, and Makepeace suddenly felt guilty about pestering her. Her face was blotchy and red, and purple bags hung under her eyes. Makepeace vaguely thought he had always considered Laura to be quite pretty. Not today, though.

'No, of course not, we can leave it till you are better, but I know the sarge would appreciate it if you could outline what happened. Because Jill, of course, didn't make it.'

Tears rolled down Laura's face. 'It was so awful, and so unexpected. I was just trying to help. Jill asked me to untangle the sequins and threads that she had just dumped in the box after she finished the costumes, and so I took it all out, but it was too hard. The sequins were cutting my fingers, and Jill said to do what I could and then when it got too difficult, cut the thread. I picked up the scissors ...' she stopped, gulped, and swallowed before going on. 'And as Jill came in with the tea, I went to help her, because she was balancing the biscuits and two cups, and I could see the Tim Tams were melting against the hot cups. You know how easy it is to melt those chocolate biscuits. And though they are great when melted … anyway, I tripped on the stupid sequins and the scissors just went flying.'

Makepeace was scribbling as quickly as he could. 'So, the scissors might have your fingerprints on them?'

'I don't know, there was so much blood, my fingerprints might have rubbed off. It was horrible. They went right through her neck, and blood was everywhere. I tried to remember my first aid, and I pulled the scissors out so I could roll her over and do CPR, but it made it worse.'

'And then what happened?'

'Rosie arrived, then I rang triple zero and she told me I shouldn't have touched the scissors, but it was too late. Jill's blood got all over me, and I vomited as well.' Laura shuddered.

'We'll leave it there, Laura. I can see it's really upsetting, and what you've given us will be enough for us to start with. It sounds like a horrible, dreadful accident.'

Laura smiled gratefully at him and closed her eyes. Makepeace stood watching her for a few seconds, then quietly left the room as a nurse bustled in and checked Laura's temperature and blood pressure, adjusted the drip, then left her in peace.

***

It was some days before Laura was released and up and about again. Her arm took a few more days to heal, and her spirit took even longer. Makepeace had visited her at home, extracted more details from her and obtained copies of the doctor's reports. She seemed to have lost her usual energy and sat quietly on the couch.

Makepeace was optimistic that there would be no further action. 'The sarge doesn't seem to think you had any motive for wanting to harm Jill,' he said as he was leaving after taking yet another statement.

Laura had been about to close the front door, but at this she swung it open again and followed Makepeace out towards his car. 'What? Of course not! Why, I couldn't have done without Jill for the launch. The costumes were magnificent, and she did them all without complaining. Why would I have it in for her?'

Makepeace blushed. 'I shouldn't have said anything,' he mumbled. He tried to open the car door, but Laura stood in front of him.

'I wish you would say more. What on earth is going on?'

'Well … oh, it's nothing really.'

'Makepeace. I'm not letting you leave until you tell me what's going on.'

He sighed. Laura could be very bossy when she wanted to be. 'You must not, I mean *not* ever tell anyone. Can you promise?'

Laura glared at him but didn't speak. She raised an eyebrow and encouraged him to continue.

'Jill used to be married, you knew that?' Laura nodded. Makepeace went on, 'Her ex was a man called Claud. Claud Fothergill.'

Laura put a hand on the car door to steady herself. Makepeace held her other arm and guided her back inside.

'I gather that name isn't altogether unknown to you.' He spoke gently and softly. Laura shook her head.

'I do know that name. And you know I knew that name.'

They both sat. 'We had to interview anyone with a close connection to Jill. His name appeared in her paperwork. When we caught up with him, he was totally covered with an alibi, but when the incident was described to him, he declared that he knew you from, well, a long time ago.'

Laura bit her lips and stared out the window. 'It was indeed a long time ago.' She looked back at the police officer. 'Did he tell you how I came to know him? And that I have not been in contact with him since I left town?' He nodded.

'Yes, he told us about what happened, and how you had made the choice you made. He seemed a little sad, to tell you the truth.'

'We were both young. A relationship would never have worked. I try not to think about it, but sometimes it comes back when I least expect it. I had no idea he was Jill's ex. What a small world.'

'I gather he had been trying to reconcile with her a few months ago but she wouldn't have anything to do with him.'

'She never talked about it. Any conversation about partners was always very brief and she seemed to shut it down.'

'Anyway, you can see why the sarge wanted to make sure you didn't hold a grudge and were getting back at him by attacking his ex. It does sound a bit far-fetched, but we were just dotting i's and crossing t's.'

Laura stood again, and this time, she allowed Makepeace to exit. He turned as he reached the car. 'Remember, you promised not to say a thing.'

Chapter 16

The scattering of Ned's ashes was a poignant event. It had taken considerable time for the family to plan the ceremony. No one could quite agree on the time, the place, or who should be invited. In the meantime, the ashes, in a plastic urn, had been sitting on the mantelpiece of Ned's sister's house, in a town about forty kilometres away. In the end it became, as most things in Cowagulac, a village affair. The residents, or what remained of them, had come together on a morning when a watery sun was forcing its way through the clouds. The urn was standing, resplendent, on a red cloth that had been draped, somewhat fittingly, over a tree stump. A haystack in the valley was buffeted by unseen winds, its green canvas covering billowing out like a spinnaker.

Cars were pulling up to the clearing some fifty metres away from the cliff and disgorging their solemnly clad occupants. Ned's sister had arrived earlier, along with the celebrant who was to officiate the ceremony. The first of the villagers to arrive were Laura and Aunt Rosie, then Ivy and Geranium, who had stopped to pick up Ingrid. Lancelot and

Klaus straggled along with a few others who muttered about milking cows or baling hay. The last car door slammed, and the group gathered quietly around the decorated tree stump.

The wind attacked them from the valley as though it was bored of playing with the haystack and had come to see what other fun might lie on land. Skirts were whipped into unseemly positions on large rumps, hats were held on with one hand, and coat buttons were hastily fastened. The celebrant stepped forward, shouting to be heard over the now gale force wind.

'Friends and relatives of the late Ned Christophers. Thank you for attending this service today. We come to pay our respects to Ned, a sculptor who was unique within the entire valley, a man who used his artistry to create public works which were dramatic and unforgettable.'

'Just like the manner of his death,' hissed Ingrid out of the corner of her mouth.

'Shh,' Laura frowned. 'Have some respect.' Ingrid raised her eyebrows and refrained from reminding Laura of her role in the untimely passing of Ned.

A loud sob from Auntie Rosie drew Laura's attention and she spread a comfortingly large arm around Rosie's thin figure. 'You're just skin and bone,' she murmured. 'What's happened to you?' The celebrant droned on, though only the family were paying rapt attention. Rosie's figure was enveloped by Laura, who was wrapped in the voluminous coat she always wore when the weather dropped below twenty-three degrees. Laura was not one to tolerate the cold. However, she slipped the coat off and draped it over Rosie, where it hung like an oversized garment on a skinny mannequin. Rosie looked up at Laura, her eyes seeming to beseech her to understand, to comfort. In turn, Laura's eyes filled with tears which were rapidly dispersed by the wind.

The celebrant droned on while the congregation shifted from foot to foot and waited for the denouement. No one had forgotten the unpleasantness of the discussion about disposing of Ned's ashes, and there was an unspoken division between Ned's sister and the villagers, only observable through the studious avoidance of eye contact between the two sides.

'Poor Ned,' sniffed Aunt Rosie, now feeling uncomfortably warm with Laura's coat wrapped as tightly as swaddling clothes around her.

'There, there,' the timeless comforting statement from Laura did nothing to stem the flow of tears dripping constantly from Rose's eyes, and the unsightly globs of snot that leaked from her nose. After a monologue listing the most well-known of Ned's sculptures, the tones of the celebrant rose, and the final words were spoken.

'And so, we scatter the ashes of Ned, a major force in our art community, over the valley from which he drew his inspiration, and we ask the Creator of all that is good in the world to take our friend Ned to rest in peace for ever. Ladies and gentlemen, thank you for coming, and we now ask you to form a line across the cliff and assist in the sprinkling of the ashes.

Everyone obediently, albeit somewhat stiffly, moved into a ragged line near the clifftop. The clouds were scudding across the sky and an ominous grey pall hung near the horizon. Rosie, looking into the valley, saw the trees bend double in the wind, and felt her eyelashes almost torn from her face. She tried to move free from Laura in preparation to take the plastic urn and participate in sprinkling some ash. However, it was now apparent that bits of Ned were being blown back into everyone's faces and soiling the assortment of 'best' clothes that had been selected for funeral wear. Grey ash covered Laura's coat, and she tutted as she brushed her hand down the fabric, making dust and ash fly further into the crowd.

A sudden swirl of wind lifted people almost off their feet. It did, in fact, lift Rosie off her feet, and she was propelled forward right to the cliff edge.

'Help!' She called out, but the words were torn from her by the wind and sent scattering.

'Rosie, I'm coming!' Laura dropped her bag and ran forward two steps, grabbing at Rosie's outstretched arm as she was pulled ever closer to the edge.

'Take my hand Rosie, grab it, hang on.' People close to them had noticed what was happening and, suddenly, a crowd had gathered, everyone talking in louder and louder voices as Rosie was virtually sucked away from Laura's outstretched hand. It seemed for a second, which stretched into eternity, that she had succeeded at clinging to Laura, but then her body was whisked over the cliff, tumbling like a prize acrobat, and the last view people had was of her snowy white undies as her dress was inelegantly blown over her head.

'Laura!' Rosie's voice petered out as she bounced her way down the cliff with sickening crunches and thumps until there was silence. The wind immediately dropped away to almost nothing.

The rest of Ned's ashes were thrown over as well, as people peered over the cliff. The plastic urn rolled down the hill, bouncing, spilling its remaining contents untidily. Ash rose in clouds, causing sneezing and coughing in the otherwise quiet crowd.

First to speak was Laura. 'Well, someone, do something. Joe, get your tractor, we can send a rope down to Rosie. She might be alive, might just have a broken leg or arm.' But the silence from below and the sight of the broken body didn't really leave room for any doubt. Rosie was dead.

***

The death shocked the village. Rosie was such a central character. The coffee shop in the CCCC looked forlorn and dusty, even after only two days without Rosie's constant polishing of the glass display cabinet.

Laura stopped by to remove the limp croissants and curling sandwiches. She had experienced rat and mouse plagues in the village and had no desire to repeat them. It seemed in bad taste to reopen the café, but it had to be admitted that the CCCC valued the income that flowed from it.

She called on an elderly couple from neighbouring Maniagallup, who she thought would not be freaked out by taking over a dead woman's business. They were more than happy to run the café on a part time basis. Olive was an experienced cook, and Bill a retired accountant so it was with a lighter heart that Laura handed over the keys.

'People might be a bit slow in coming back, but give it time,' she said, heaving herself off the chair and returning her cup to the counter. 'They all know about Rosie, and we are planning to have the memorial right here in a week or so. Will you be able to cater for that?'

Olive and Bill assured Laura all would be in train for the event. 'Just one question,' Bill stopped Laura as she picked up her bag. 'What about the safe? There's one in the back room, and we don't know the combination. It would be good to be able to lock away any spare cash till we can get to the bank.'

'I'll have a look,' Laura ducked, with difficulty, under the counter flap and walked into the back room. 'Hmm, I know Rosie once told me what it was. Let me think.' She sat in front of the metal box and waited for inspiration.

Most people in Cowagulac knew that Laura used the same password for everything, but she was blithely unaware that this left her vulnerable to being defrauded. 'No one in Cowagulac would be that dishonest,' she had been heard to say, and no matter how much people tried to explain to her that the internet was not just a local structure, Laura maintained her stout defence of *TimTam1*. Her lips tightening, Laura hopefully entered *TimTam1* on the keypad, but there was no response. She could picture the occasion when Rosie had told her the password. The little woman was rushing around carrying coffee cups and hinting that Laura should leave her kingdom.

Then it came back to her. *Ah, yes, I remember. White and one, like most people ordered their coffee, but because there weren't enough numbers she had to abbreviate it.* Laura entered *wite1* and the lock clicked. 'There.' Laura sighed with satisfaction.

Moments later, Olive swung open the door to the safe. 'Oh, there's some papers in here. You'd better take charge of them'. She stepped back, and Laura pulled out a thick envelope.

'Thank you, Olive. Now, are you okay with that code? I'm afraid I don't know how to change it.'

'No that's fine. We trust you not to come and rob us of the small change.'

When she got home, Laura looked at the contents of the envelope she had taken from the safe. 'I think I need to contact Rosie's solicitor,' she said to herself.

Chapter 17

Mr Drybeck, Rosie's solicitor, sent an email to Laura and the CCCC committee.

Dear Ms Adams,

It read, in standard 12-point Times New Roman.

As you may be aware, Rosie's recent death necessitates the distribution of her estate. Our firm has been appointed executors, and, following the instructions given to us, we intend to hold a formal reading of the Will. It was Rosie's specific request that this be held at the CCCC, and the whole village invited. This will occur on the twenty-second of this month, at 11 am. The reading will be followed by a light lunch. Rosie left instructions about the catering that will be required.

Yours sincerely,
Adam Drybeck.

Laura sat back and blinked rapidly to disperse the uncalled-for tears. She had never really liked Rosie, perhaps they were too much alike, but the memory of her bouncing down the cliff, upstaging the scattering of Ned's ashes, would not leave her head. She held no grudges that her favourite coat was ruined by the fall. She felt slightly uneasy at having installed Olive and Bill into the café without a thought of what Rosie's Will might dictate, but was comforted by the knowledge that the café itself was in the CCCC and was not Rosie's to distribute. The goodwill maybe, but not the physical layout and the chattels. Life was complex sometimes.

She got busy and contacted anyone who she could think of. It was as good an opportunity for gossip as any, and although she had no knowledge of the contents of the Will to pass on – since the envelope in the safe had been sealed with wax and the name of the solicitor written on the front – it looked like there would be at least twenty people there, so she let Olive know to prepare. If she had been thinking straight, she would have asked Mr Drybeck about the arrangements.

✱✱✱

It was a cool but fine day for the memorial service. Laura arrived an hour early to oversee the placing of chairs and tables and check that Olive had things ready. She need not have worried. Bill had done the physical preparations and Olive had sandwiches, party pies, sushi – Laura thought that sushi would not be popular in this community, but that maybe she could take some home for lunch tomorrow – and little cakes. How much she would miss seeing Ned, and Jill for that matter.

She had more or less got over her adoration of Ned. Not that it had been easy at first. He seemed to have permeated many of her waking thoughts, but now the romantic anticipations and hopes had been washed away in the memory of the spurting blood from his neck. How foolish she felt about that silly spider now. Luckily, no one really knew that part of the story. Her reputation as a competent organiser would be shot to pieces. And if Klaus knew, he wouldn't say anything.

Ivy and Geranium were the first to arrive. Laura wasn't at all surprised about this, as they had not only become part of the community but were also extremely fond of gossip. They ordered coffees and sat down to talk to Laura.

'Our workshop preparation is going well,' Ivy commented between sips. 'We have learned some interesting background of people here, and once we add some illustrations and photos, Geranium and I think it will be a lovely record of the local community.'

'It was a bit of a challenge sorting out Klaus's grammar, but my, doesn't he have an interesting story! I was wondering if anyone would know what Rosie was referring to when she talked about her parents and a UFO event?'

Laura shook her head. 'That was between Klaus and Rosie, so you might get more information from him. Speaking of Klaus, here he is.'

Ivy turned to see Klaus walking into the café, his magnificent mane of hair brushed to gleaming. Ivy made as though to get up and speak to him, but Geranium put a restraining hand on her arm. 'Not now,' she whispered. 'I'll try and catch him later. Maybe he would be interested in my idea about a workshop about local poisonous plants and their antidotes. He is, after all, a genuine naturalist and vegetarian.'

'He doesn't seem to have a partner,' Ivy said, looking at Klaus with a smile and raised eyebrows. 'Maybe we should ask him over for a cup of nettle tea with bush honey.' Klaus turned his back on the ladies and took a seat.

Karen arrived, with several beloved dogs who sat around outside, frowning through their shaggy fringes. Lancelot, Ingrid, Dora and a host of others – who were just coming for the free feed – gradually filed in.

Mr Drybeck pulled up opposite the front door in a Mercedes, obviously finding the short walk from the car park to be beyond his capacity. He strode to the front of the café and cleared his throat. The murmur of the crowd fell away, leaving silence except for the commercial fridge switching on and off. Olive slid the serving hatch door closed and the fridge noise faded into the background.

'Can you all hear me?' Mr Drybeck's voice came out in a squeaky kind of treble. He cleared his throat and began again, this time more confidently.

'I am required, as Rosie's executor, to call this meeting of interested parties, both to read the Will, as well as another document which my client attached to the Will. This I will do without further comment.' There was a murmur among the audience, and an air of puzzlement.

'Firstly, the Will. Rosie left a simple Will. It reads as follows: I leave the café business to Laura Adams, who has always taken a great interest in its success. Any goods and chattels I leave to Ivy Vine and Geranium Golightly jointly, as they have been the least inquisitive of the people who live in this village. Any monies and bank accounts I leave to the Cowagulac Community Cultural Centre management. I wish to be buried in the Cowagulac cemetery, where there is a family plot.'

Mr Drybeck looked up and coughed lightly. 'As you can see, it is a simple Will, and I will be in contact with the named parties in the near future. I now propose to read the attached document.'

He continued, 'I am entrusting this document to my solicitor, to be read to the Cowagulac community after my death. For many years I have lived in this village and seen a number of disasters, and near disasters, befall it. I am hopeful, at the time of writing, that we are on a path to a bright future. The Community Cultural Centre and the residents appear to have developed a plan which will provide a career path for young people, encouraging them to remain here and join in family businesses, succeed in farming and be part of the community.' There was a smattering of applause, probably started by Lancelot, but it soon died away.

'As an elder stateswoman of the community, I feel it behoves me to offer some advice. Of course, some of the people I would have given wise counsel to are dead. Their sudden and violent deaths caused me to rethink my small estate. I should have told Ned that his wood carvings really were terrible, and he should find a different career, though no one would employ him with all those gold earrings. And Jill, I would have advised to go on a strict diet. I myself have never had a problem with overeating, but I do sympathise with people who do.' The words sounded exactly as though it was Rosie there in person, and a few comments could be heard from the crowd.

'Sounds like she had a fair few opinions, our Rosie,' came from Ingrid to Dora.

'I d-d-didn't know she had such a good vocabulary,' Lancelot hissed to Laura.

'She used lots of big words, but I don't think she knew what half of them meant.' Laura retaliated.

The solicitor waited till there was silence, then went on.

'Ingrid, I wish you all the best with your attempts to get Dora on the charts. I think you have done a magnificent job with – let's face it – not very promising material. Dora, keep working. Practice makes perfect, you know. My parents told me that every time I refused to do my piano scales. Karen, I strongly suggest a smaller breed of dog. Not everyone likes being licked in the face and slobbered on. Laura, maybe you can help your sister make better choices. I spent hours cleaning the café after a visit from the hounds, and Laura, I expect you to maintain that level of cleanliness. I hope Mr Drybeck will check on that from time to time.'

'Well,' an indignant exclamation issued forth from Laura, 'who does she think she is? I've a good mind not to take on the café ownership.' Ivy patted her hand.

'Rosie is dead remember, love. No need to take offence.'

Mr Drybeck cleared his throat and the comments subsided. There was, somehow, even more to be read.

'Lancelot, my old friend. I do believe there are some good speech therapists who could improve that stammer of yours. You do really well on the radio despite that, though I sometimes shudder when I listen to how you struggle. It isn't too late. And Klaus, what a strange lifestyle you lead. I really don't know how you survive in this challenging countryside. You and your UFOs! I remember when you got me to sit out all night waiting, and then I claimed the next morning to have seen them. But that was after you gave me some very odd tasting, dried, shrivelled fungi to eat. I think I might have been hallucinating. And no, Klaus, my parents were not kidnapped and killed by aliens. And if they were, I am sure I will already know about it in the place that has been reserved for me after death, wherever that may be. As for your lichens and vegetables and witchetty grubs or whatever you eat, that's another story. But one thing that does impress me is your skill in numerology. That is quite extraordinary. I've heard you tell futures using that. I've seen you arrange your diet by adding up the numbers of letters and choosing morning tea from my delectable cake range based solely on the number, not whether you like to eat it. I can only assume there's something a bit odd in your mind. Just remember my words and keep on adding up the numbers. After all, there's not *mushroom* for error.' Mr Drybeck struggled with this written joke, not seeming to get the point until there was a small titter in the audience. He looked up.

'I've nearly finished, ladies and gentlemen, and then we shall have refreshments.' Laura slipped out of her seat and went through to the kitchen to alert Olive. 'Finally, I want to say that you perhaps are seeing a different side of me today. For years I have stayed silent and tolerated a whole lot of things that annoyed me, and I must say, just writing this has made me feel fantastic, even though I'm sure I will be modifying it before it's read out, since it is to accompany my Will and I don't plan to die any time soon. Farewell, villagers, and I'm sure you will be much happier if you take Aunt Rosie's advice.'

Mr Drybeck shuffled the papers together and made a steeple with his long fingers. 'That concludes the meeting today, but you are all welcome to stay for a cup of tea. If I could see the legatees briefly that would be helpful.'

The serving counter was mobbed by a crowd of unnamed locals who had come for the free feed, but the ones who Rosie had lacerated with her razor-sharp tongue sat, for the most part, stunned. Klaus made a point of pushing in at the counter and ordering a cream cake, which he dropped on the floor and ground in with his boot before stalking off. He muttered under his breath, 'Darn woman. Cream cake adds up to sixty, perfectly divisible. I could even just eat the cream – forty – or the cake – twenty – but I'm not going to let her get the better of me.'

Laura gazed out the window, eyes glistening with tears. Her village was falling apart. Too many people were dying. Despite her young age, she had experienced so much death. People were not dying in the right order. The old, followed by the young. That's what should happen.

Lancelot clamped his lips together as though trying to prevent a stammer from escaping and made a quick exit to his car.

Ingrid hurried Dora out and could be heard encouraging her with, 'My dear, you have been such a recording star, we don't need to worry about an embittered old spinster who was jealous of your success.'

Ivy and Geranium watched the reactions with mild amusement mixed with genuine concern for the people who had become their friends.

Karen went to her car and let out the two dogs for a wee, then knelt and patted their big bony heads, resting her forehead on the soft fur and encircled them in her arms.

Altogether, it was a dramatic day.

Chapter 18

Ingrid sighed. It was wonderful, she conceded that Dora – Velvet, rather – had been asked to present her new single in Balsham, but recreating the launch at the CCCC was impossible now that Ned was dead. Who else would fit his costume, let alone his role? And Velvet's own costume was the worse for wear. The only choice was to have only Velvet in costume. The brilliant red and blue of the feathered outfit would make for great local television and Ingrid confidently anticipated the front page of the local paper. Anyway, she thought, it might be more effective for sales to just have the artist herself, rather than the distractions of the other animals.

Ingrid checked the time. Velvet was late. It was bad enough that she, Ingrid, had to try to repair the rosella costume using a needle and thread – and goodness knows how she would manage that – but to have to wait for Velvet to be her usual, tardy self was just too much.

Just as Ingrid pulled out her phone to call Velvet, a chorus of crunching gravel accompanied by a cloud of dust rising voluminously over the front gate indicated the arrival of Velvet's car.

Ingrid found herself sinking in a sea of apologies, as she ushered Velvet through the front door. Swiftly, she issued instructions for Velvet to change into the costume immediately.

It was a very forlorn rosella that reappeared – missing feathers, a claw hanging precariously from Velvet's right big toe, even a coffee stain on her half-detached left wing.

'I'm so sorry, I should have taken more care, I know.' Velvet wiped away a tear with a grubby hand. 'I just loved wearing it so much.'

'No tears now, we just have to fix it,' Ingrid responded. 'It's nothing patience and a bit of ingenuity can't repair. Now come a little closer and I'll start pinning.'

'Thank you for rescuing me,' mumbled Velvet, shuffling forward. Her progress, however, was somewhat impeded. The hanging claw had caught in Ingrid's shag pile rug. Neither the claw's last threads nor the rug's errant loops gave way, despite Velvet's determined tugs.

'Here, let me help you,' said Ingrid, kneeling close to the problem.

'Oh! Oh! Oh!' A howl came from Velvet.

Neither could recall quite what happened next. All Velvet remembered was one last desperate tug, then an almighty fall, the glass top of the coffee table shattering and piercing her leg. She fell on top of Ingrid, crying out in pain.

'Ugh, Velvet, get off.' gasped Ingrid, trying to push Velvet away. This proved painful – Ingrid learned later that she had two fractured ribs.

Velvet wailed, pointing to her bloodied right leg.

'It will be all right, it just needs a few stitches, I'm sure,' panted Ingrid.

Velvet shook her head frantically. 'It's not the cut, I think my leg is broken, no, I'm sure it's broken. Can you call an ambulance, please?'

In an instant – by Cowagulac Community Ambulance Service standards – that seemed like an eternity, both Ingrid and Velvet were made comfortable for the short ride to Cowagulac Community Health Service and the adjoining Bush Nursing Hospital.

***

Ingrid arranged to postpone the big appearance in Balsham. Dora was visited by Laura and Lancelot, and Ingrid, too, proved a faithful visitor over the coming days. Initially, she went to the hospital but later to Velvet's home. She had been released after her leg had been bandaged and her ribs were less painful. Velvet didn't blame Ingrid at all for the incident.

'No, Ingrid, you were only trying to help. I couldn't have sewn the costume up again, and you arranged for me to appear on the media wearing it. It was my fault for wearing it so much.' Ingrid soothed her in order to avoid a ping-pong of fault allocation.

On this particular Thursday, she set out with plans to celebrate Velvet's ongoing recovery, even, in a moment of recklessness splashing out on a bottle of gin for victory G&Ts. But Velvet looked awful and refused a cup of tea, let alone a G&T.

'Velvet dear, you can't let your spirits collapse like this. You've been doing so well. What's happened?'

'I don't know Ingrid, I feel like I'm coming down with the flu. And my leg's just throbbing. It wasn't like this yesterday.'

But Ingrid wasn't listening. Instead, she was staring at Velvet's right leg. Red swollen skin swelled out over the bandage.

'Velvet, this is infected!' she said. 'Are you sure you didn't notice anything yesterday?'

'Well, maybe just a bit of swelling again …'

'We have to get you back to hospital.'

'Please not that, Ingrid, I hated being there.'

'I'm sure you did,' retorted Ingrid. 'But at least they'll know how to treat it.'

'No, I won't go back there, seriously, I won't,' Velvet insisted. 'I could be right, you realise, it could just be the flu. You ache all over with flu. I'm just lucky only my leg hurts so far. I'll just keep it raised, and I'm sure the swelling will go down. If it doesn't, I'll go to the doctor.' This was met with a long pause.

'Very well,' Ingrid agreed with obvious apprehension. 'But we will see how you are in the morning. Even if it's the flu, you should probably see a doctor. And I don't like the look of that swelling and redness, regardless. Keep that leg elevated.'

'All right,' said Velvet meekly, avoiding eye contact. 'If you say so.'

With unexpected tenderness, Ingrid bent forward and kissed Velvet's brow. 'Take care then, and I'll see you in the morning.'

Next morning, Ingrid called round as promised. She was worried, really worried, that she had given in to Velvet's protests too readily and should have insisted on her seeing a doctor.

Possessed by such thoughts, she knocked on the front door and waited. And waited. Then she knocked again. There was no response from within.

'Velvet! Velvet!' she shouted. Still no response. Even more uneasy, Ingrid rounded the side of Velvet's house to approach the bathroom window, hoping to hear the shower running, but there was only silence. Ingrid reached for her phone and rang Velvet, but the phone rang out, unanswered. Finally, she tried the front door and breathed a sigh of relief as it opened without effort.

'Velvet,' she called, 'where are you?' But she already felt there would be no answer. Something in the almost funereal silence made her expect this. Slowly, reluctantly, overwhelmed with dread, Ingrid pushed open the bedroom door.

Velvet lay lifeless on the bed.

In what seemed to be an all too familiar occurrence of recent times, the police and ambulance arrived. Constable Makepeace took Ingrid's statement, while the ambulance officers declared Dora to be dead. Ingrid was in shock. She was working to help her new star find a niche in the statewide – maybe countrywide – market, and instead had killed her, or as good as. She asked the police officer if she was in trouble.

'It was my coffee table. When she tripped, she fell on it and shattered the glass. If it hadn't been for that, she wouldn't have been in hospital in the first place.'

'If what you are saying is true, miss, then you've done nothing wrong. Her leg got infected; you aren't responsible for that, I'm sure.'

Ingrid sighed and wiped her eyes. 'No, I visited her but had to wait my turn. Laura was there already.' Ingrid was a little surprised at the vindictive tone in her voice. 'Oh, I'm sorry, I don't mean anything, it's just that I'm upset.'

'Perfectly understandable, miss. But I'll take a statement from Miss Laura after I've spoken to the sarge. You get along now; there's nothing more you can do here.'

Gratefully, Ingrid climbed into her car and backed out, missing the police car by mere inches. She felt the need for some sympathy and headed to Ivy's place. She liked Geranium but found Ivy slightly the softer of the two.

Both ladies were in the loungeroom, cups of tea on small tables.

'Ingrid, come on in, you look dreadful.' Without speaking, Geranium bustled out to the kitchen and brought in frosted glasses of water along with the teapot. Ingrid found she was very thirsty and gulped down the first glass of water before Geranium had even poured the tea.

'Sit down, poor girl, and tell us what's happened. We did see the police car racing past earlier. Is everything all right?' Geranium put two spoons of sugar in the cup before stirring it and handing it to Ingrid.

Ivy leaned forward. 'Only tell us if you want to, my dear.'

Ingrid sipped the tea but quickly put it down on the table. She didn't normally take sugar and found it a little sickly.

'It's Velvet. I found her dead in her house. From blood poisoning, I think.'

The two older ladies tutted and twittered around till Ingrid had told them the whole story. Silence fell. Ivy and Geranium seemed to know each other so well that they could anticipate what the other was going to say, and it was a bit disconcerting that they would sometimes finish each other's sentences. Ingrid sometimes felt confused about who was actually speaking.

'Do the police think …' Ivy began.

'… that it was an accident? They aren't thinking …'

'… that it was your fault, surely?'

Ingrid waited till there was a pause. 'Constable Makepeace said I didn't do anything wrong, but he was going to talk to Laura.'

Geranium took the lead this time, 'Why Laura? I'm sure lots of other people …'

'… visited Dora in hospital, didn't they?'

'No, I don't think so. I didn't have time to tell many people, and to be honest, Velvet wasn't that popular.'

Ivy and Geranium exchanged glances.

'I'm sure we would have gone,' Ivy interjected.

'If we had known, that is.'

'Dreadful thing to be in hospital …'

'… by yourself.'

'Do have some more tea. I dried the leaves myself. It's all herbal.'

Ingrid handed over her cup for a refill, having swallowed the sweet liquid and finding it not as bad as she first thought, in fact vaguely comforting. 'Laura probably found out Velvet was there from someone at the hospital. She knows lots of people. I didn't tell her, at any rate.'

'Well, I suppose we will have to wait and see whether there is to be an inquest. After all, she had been in medical care, so perhaps there won't be a need.' This entire sentence was uttered by Geranium who sat back, seemingly exhausted by the effort.

'Oh, I do hope not. That would be horrid for everyone,' Ivy responded.

***

Lancelot frowned as he added Dora's death to his Excel chart. If he was to keep up his regular interview segments on *Tragedies in Cowagulac* he would have to find someone to interview.

Some days later, the Coroner, Steph Allen, ruled the death to be an accident, and cleared the hospital of any negligence.

Dora was dead, but through no fault of anyone.

For as long as she had lived in Cowagulac, Dora had made no reference to a family, so it was a surprise when a shiny, black Range Rover drove into the village a week after her death. A man in a tight blue suit and a woman in white trousers and a matching blazer emerged from the vehicle. Laura was passing at the time, and the woman held out a hand to stop her.

'Could you direct me to the police station?'

Laura raised her eyebrows. 'Well yes, though it's not exactly a tourist attraction.'

The woman, tall and bleached, fixed a steely gaze on Laura. Normally impervious to the opinions of others, Laura felt as though a blast of cold air had been directed at her.

'Norman and I are here to arrange for our niece, Dora, to be buried. We have driven down from Noosa, but we will be staying in Balsham. I require the police station or the town hall.'

Laura was taken aback. 'Oh, of course. I'm so sorry for your loss. We all miss Dora dreadfully. I'm Laura, one of Dora's friends.'

'Laura?' There was a distinctly hostile tone in the tall woman's voice. 'I seem to recall Dora mentioned a Laura. Said something about how bossy she was.'

Laura gulped. 'Well, I suppose some people do see me that way. I try to organise things, you know.'

'It seems a pity you didn't organise for the repair of my niece's theatrical outfit. In that case, she might be still with us.'

The criticism seemed unfair, and, despite her best intentions, Laura fired back, 'I am sorry we didn't get to meet you at the launch of the recording. I'm sure Dora would have been happy to introduce us.' She hoped to sting the woman into some feelings of guilt but was disappointed.

'We were in Antarctica at the time. But I'm sure, had she lived, there would have been many more successful recordings to follow. Now, perhaps you could give us directions.'

At that moment the police car drove slowly past, and Laura waved it down and, having introduced the couple to Constable Makepeace, she hastened down the street to continue her shopping, regretting not being able to learn more about Dora's past from the somewhat intimidating woman.

Chapter 19

The smell of frying mushrooms wafted throughout the house, and Klaus found his mouth watering in anticipation. Today was to be his third attempt at astral travelling. He thought he was getting much better at it, though all the text references to a 'silver cord' and 'vibrations' worried him. He didn't feel any attachment to his spirit via any cord at all, and, as far as he recalled, there were no vibrations. Maybe this time he would have better luck.

There was nothing in the literature about whether to eat prior to travelling but he figured it was better to undertake a journey on a full stomach. And maybe with a bit of wine to relax his spirit even more. After all, if you were going on a train journey, or a road trip, you wouldn't want to stop at a roadhouse or fast-food outlet as soon as the journey had got underway.

Having eaten some fried cabbage – by itself cabbage was a twenty-one, but when fried it became fifty-eight which was just satisfactory where steamed would not work at all – with beans and, of course, mushrooms, he washed the few dishes and moved softly to the lounge room. He picked up his quartz crystal, bought at great expense from *Healers R Us* in the Main Street of Balsham. He had considered at length whether to buy it online, but since that world was just as much of a mystery to him as astral travelling, he went there in person. That was a story for another time but, suffice it to say, it was highly embarrassing. He now ordered any further goods online.

He set his mobile going with some instructions for getting the journey underway. It was a pleasant female voice, and he took a comfortable position on the couch and tried to follow the guide.

'Breathe gently and deeply, and close your eyes.' Soft, but twangy music played underneath the voice. 'Place the crystal on top of your third eye, just above your eyebrows. This will speed up the vibrations. Breathe deeply, now.' There was silence on the recording for so long that Klaus nearly stopped his journey before it had started to check whether the battery had gone flat. Just in time, however, the music started again, followed by the voice. 'Now feel the vibrations. Your head is clear and light. Colours will appear in your vision. Gold, silver, deep, deep purple, white. As these appear and become stronger, take the crystal from your head and place it on your chest, or hold it in your hand. The crystal has high energy. It will fight and disband the low vibrations of negative energy.'

Klaus became a trifle worried. For a start, he kept hearing noises in the kitchen, and, since he was alone in the house, he was curious as to what was making them. Then he got angry because he was desperate to go travelling. He tried to relax and breathe and feel some vibrations or see the colours, but to no avail. He returned his concentration to the voice. 'Breathe deeply and softly. Allow the vibrations to surface. Do not be afraid. Fear may drive you away from meditation and the state in which you can leave your body. Time and distance become void. Allow the vibrations to take you on the journey.'

At last! A colour streaked across his vision – gold, he was sure. He clutched the crystal on his chest and willed himself to leave his body. It was his soul, he was sure, that was ready to go. But what exactly was his soul? Never a churchgoer, Klaus almost fell off the couch in his anxiety to believe in his soul. What if he allowed some evil force in while he was out of his body? The music seemed to get louder and drown out the voice, but as this was happening, Klaus found he was looking down at his own body, half hanging off the lounge.

'It does look very uncomfortable,' he commented to himself, and contemplated whether he could lift his own legs back onto the cushions. He looked around him, amazed at the new perspective. 'Look at the dust on the top of the bookcase. Oh, and that's where my glasses went. It must have been a year since I lost those. I wonder how they got up there.' He tried to pick them up but found his hand just passing through them. Suddenly aware of what was happening, he felt a rush of air, as he landed with a thump back in his body. The recording was whirring away, not saying anything. The crystal rolled to the ground and awoke Klaus with a start.

'My goodness. I do believe I left my body.' He wriggled his fingers and toes, and tried to look around but his head wouldn't lift from the cushion.

The next thing he knew, light was coming in the window, and he felt refreshed and alert. 'My goodness, I slept the night away. And without having to go to the toilet.' Initially, Klaus counted this last point as the biggest bonus, until he discovered he had in fact, gone to the toilet. The delightful feeling of lightness and alertness dissipated, and he trudged off to change his clothes and mop up the stain on the sofa.

Chapter 20

Laura brought round the list of bookings for the dog portrait class and was quite excited as she ran her finger down the names. 'Hmm, don't know Ian Baker, or Steve Mason, or Angela Legano. Wonder if they are any good at art.'

'It isn't necessary to be good at art,' replied Karen. 'I don't care whether people can draw or not, I just want them to have fun.'

'On the other hand, it would be an asset to the CCCC if we could frame and sell some of the work. Or use it for publicity. I suppose people will take their own work home, but maybe I could donate mine. After all, I am quite talented, if I do say so myself.'

Karen raised an eyebrow. 'I didn't know you were so much into art, Laura. You've not shown great interest in my work.'

'My interest has always been more theoretical. I developed an interest in social realism and conceptual art some time ago. Of course, I didn't discuss it with you because you have your own inimitable style. More brutish, I fancy. Whereas I am more *en plein air.*'

Karen rolled her eyes. 'I just paint as I feel. I don't think any of those arty farty terms apply to my work at all.'

Karen tried to brush past Laura's highbrow view of the class, and continued to look forward to it, but she had developed a nuisance of a cold and was frustrated by having to keep mopping up a streaming nose and coughing up thick, green phlegm. She started to feel a bit chesty, and asked Laura for advice when she called in again.

'Do you think I need to go to the doctor? He's only here once a week, and by the time I started getting really miserable I'd missed the clinic.' She coughed noisily and pulled a couple of tissues from the box.

'Probably. You sound a bit asthmatic. Remember, you used to get it when you were young, but I thought you had grown out of it.'

'I've got a puffer thingy, but it's probably out of date.' She searched her handbag but couldn't find the offending item.

'You can get them at the chemist without a script. But I was wondering …' Laura paused, knowing that her next comment was going to meet with disapproval. 'I was wondering …' she repeated, but Karen sighed noisily.

'I know you were going to say maybe I'm allergic to the dogs. Well, I'm not. I've slept with Whisky Darling for nearly two years now, so surely I'd know.'

'I hope you aren't getting anaphylaxis,' Laura peered at her sister myopically.

'I don't think so. What is that?'

'You must have heard of it. It's an allergy, but your throat swells up and you die.'

Karen wrinkled her nose and frowned. 'No, I haven't got that, but I don't want it, thank you very much!'

Laura produced a bottle of eucalyptus oil from her bag and upended it on a handkerchief. 'Here, breathe this. And what I was going to say before you jumped in was that maybe you are allergic to the dander that the dogs make in different seasons. That's what I was told anyway. I believe it's especially bad on hippopotamuses and rhinos. Luckily, we don't have many of them around here.'

Karen inhaled the scent from the handkerchief deeply and gratefully. 'That feels so good. Can you leave me the bottle?'

Laura waved a hand in consent and Karen started on a bout of sneezing which continued till Laura's car had turned out of the drive.

Karen looked over the list for her class. Sixteen confirmed people, and almost half from outside the village. That was especially exciting, as it indicated her fame had spread. She had been afraid that there might be only Laura and perhaps Ivy at the class. Certainly, their names were on the list, but Karen suspected they had booked in early to ensure there were enough numbers for the class to go ahead. One name that surprised Karen was that of Lancelot. He had never struck her as someone who particularly liked dogs, and certainly not art, though he did interview many different people on his radio program so perhaps his interests had expanded. Anyway, she didn't need to worry about why people were coming, as long as they had paid.

The previous night she had washed and dried Whisky Darling, as he was to be her model for the first half of the class. He stood straight and still as she blow-dried and brushed him, raising his chin so she could comb down his throat fur. 'You are a darling. Very well named, I must say,' she crooned. When she had finished, he lay down on the rug in front of the TV and went to sleep. Karen also wanted to do that, as washing and drying even just one large dog was a big task.

One of the logistical elements of the session tomorrow worried her. The first portion of the class was to be her demonstration of how to structure and draw the outline of the animal, using Whisky Darling as her model. The class would be asked to copy her. The concerning part, however, was that, after the break, they were to bring in their own animals. These were people she didn't know. What if their dogs caused chaos and fought, or, worse still, bit someone? After Ingrid's session on legal liability, she had become quite undecided about whether to allow people to bring their own dogs, but Laura had given it the go-ahead. She knew that neither Ivy nor Lancelot had a dog, so she would lend them Whisky Darling to continue their work.

Karen gathered the kits she had prepared and called Whisky Darling to heel. Just when everything was loaded into the car, she remembered the bag of dog treats and went back inside. 'That could be the most important piece of equipment,' she thought. 'I hope all the dogs like the same treats. Oh, didn't I hear one of them was grain free? And gluten free? Or was that their owner? Oh dear, maybe I shouldn't take any treats.'

At the CCCC, she met Laura, who was already there setting out the easels and chairs. As usual, she filled the air with chatter, irritating Karen, who wanted time to settle her nerves. But she never told her older sister what to do, having learned through experience that it only made things worse. She tried to block out the monologue.

'I'm going to set a place for me as well. After all, I did get top marks in art at school, even though that was a long time ago. I thought I could draw one of our old dogs from memory. No one would know if it was realistic or not. Now, do you want these chairs in a semi-circle? And what about a little podium for your dog? He could sit up and be seen more easily. I'm sure there's one in the back room.'

Karen saw an opportunity for a moment of peace. 'Yes please, Laura, that sounds terrific. Could you get it for me?'

When Laura had disappeared behind the stage, Karen sank heavily into one of the seats and let out a sigh. Whisky Darling licked her hand. 'Yes, my poppet, I know. Auntie Laura is a chatterbox, isn't she? Does she hurt your ears, too? She's probably gone out to sketch something existentialist before the class.' Whisky Darling laid a giant paw on Karen's knee and whined. 'But there's nothing we can do about it, is there? When we get home, you and I can have a nap and recover, shall we?'

The door at the back of the stage slammed, and Karen jumped.

'I can't find it. You'll have to make do without.' From her icy tone, Karen could only conclude she had overheard the comments. Oh well, it wouldn't be the first time she had offended her sister. Laura stalked off to the café to make sure all was in order, leaving Karen to finish laying out the equipment.

Wiping nervous sweat from her face, Karen waited impatiently for the class to arrive. Two were no-shows, but they went ahead with the other fourteen, and one of the spare spaces was taken by Laura. Ivy had calmed her fears with a pleasant greeting as she arrived, and a compliment to Whisky Darling, while Lancelot had looked under his eyebrows at the dog, merely commenting, 'Well, he's big enough to see, but I think I'll need an A-three page to fit all of him on.' The class laughed dutifully at this.

'I do hope your own dogs will be okay alone for about three quarters of an hour. If you are worried, of course feel free to go and take them for a walk or a drink. When they come in after the break, please make sure they are on a lead.'

Once they had started work, Karen's nerves disappeared. 'First of all, make sure you are clear about the proportions of the animal you are drawing. Here, you see, I plan to take the whole page for my dog, so I need to divide it into thirds, as this will make it more likely that my final product is in proportion. Otherwise, you could end up with a giant head and no room for the hind quarters.' The class smiled in acknowledgement and Karen continued, now in the zone. Most people frowned with concentration as they tried to copy Karen's work. It didn't appear there were any advanced artists in the group, but Karen didn't care about that as long as they enjoyed what they were doing. With swift strokes, she outlined the dog, then, taking pastels, she coloured and shaded, until she finally put down her chalks and looked up.

'I don't normally work this quickly, but I hope you have gathered the general idea. After the break, you will paint your own animals, or of course you can continue with the one you have started. But now, make sure your workstation is tidy before you go and have a cup of tea.'

Chatter rose to almost shouting level as people walked around and admired the attempts of other class members. Only Lancelot had flipped his paper over on the easel so it was not visible and resisted all attempts to cajole him into showing it. He waited till everyone else had left for tea before he wandered out, first obtaining assurances from Karen that she would not look at his work. 'It's important to me. I might not be the world's best artist, but I don't want people gawking at my unfinished piece.'

Karen nodded and smiled. 'I'll be too busy arranging the second part of the class to worry about it.' She watched as Lancelot headed for the café and acknowledged him with a wave as he turned back to make sure she was obeying his instructions.

She was grateful when Laura brought in a cup of tea and a glass of cold water. 'Here, I hope this will help those sore ears of yours.' Karen grimaced.

'Thank you, sis. Have you looked at the work? All except Lancelot's of course. He wants his to be secret.'

'What?' Laura's tone indicated she didn't think much of Lancelot's stance. 'Well, he won't know if I have a look.'

She bowled up to his table, ignoring Karen's desperate pleas of, 'But I promised, please don't look. Some artists get very upset when their work is seen before it is finished.'

But Laura had already turned the paper over and was snorting with laughter. 'My God, come and look at this. No wonder he didn't want anyone to see it. It's no better than kindergarten standard, look!' And she swung the paper around so Karen could see it, just as Lancelot appeared in the doorway. He strode forward and ripped the paper out of her hands.

'I *told* you I wanted to keep this private. You and your sister, you're as bad as each other. You promised, Karen. I'll know better than to t-t-trust you another time.' He crumpled the paper into a ball and threw it towards the bin as he strode from the room. 'I'm going to write tomorrow's editorial about this.'

There was silence except for the distant chatter and clatter of cups from the café. 'Now look what you've done.' Karen was close to tears. 'Not only have we to explain away Lancelot's absence, but everyone who listens to CowRadio will know about this tomorrow.'

Laura put an arm around Karen's shoulders. 'Don't worry, old thing. I'll go and explain it to him after the class. He needs a bit of time to cool down.' Karen shrugged off Laura's attempt to console her.

'This is my class, and you came close to ruining it.'

People were starting to file back in with their animals, and in a few minutes the room was in chaos, filled with barks, whimpers, stern commands, tangled leads, shouts, and confusion. No one seemed to notice Lancelot was missing and the second half was a great success.

Karen's fear of savage, biting dogs disrupting the class soon dissipated as friendly spoodles sniffed the bottoms of heelers and greyhounds, while German Shepherds inspected the Cavalier King Charles. Everyone had loosened up, and there was relaxed chatter and laughter as they tried to get their dogs to stay as still as Whisky Darling. All too soon, the time was up, and Karen's sign-up sheet for the next class was full as everyone enthusiastically promised to return.

'Before you all leave, I was wondering if you would like a small bit of competition. If you would take a short break, Laura and I will put the pictures at random on the easels, and when you return, you can have a guess at which dog and owner belongs to which artwork.' Everyone was enthusiastic about this idea.

Laura was in stitches over some of the artistic renditions. 'I can't even tell which dog this is,' she said, pointing for a grey blob in the middle of the page.

'Silly, that's the greyhound!'

'How on earth can you make a greyhound out of that?' Laura held the painting upside down and shook her head.

'The collar. See, it's diamantes. At least, I think those white splodges are meant to be diamantes.'

'Okay smarty-pants, then what is this one?' The painting looked like a mixture between a horse and a giraffe. 'Easy. It's the heeler.'

When Laura looked at Karen under lowered brows, Karen had the grace to blush. 'Oh, all right, I saw her drawing it.'

A few minutes later, the class filed back into the room, clutching paper and pen to write down their guesses. The competition was an idea which had come suddenly to Karen, so she hadn't planned how to finish it, but, before long, everyone was laughing and pointing out the features of each painting and how far removed it was from the dog it was meant to portray.

'We should get the dogs to pose under the correct portrait,' Ivy suggested but the idea was lost in the bustle.

Laura clapped her hands, and the class gradually quietened. 'Thank you all for coming, and I'd like to thank Karen, too, for her excellent tuition and organisation.' A round of applause indicated that most people agreed with this, and the afternoon came to a pleasant close.

'I guess you will go home and have a nap now, since my talking is so draining,' said Laura.

'I'm sorry Laura. I didn't mean anything, you know that. I was just very stressed about the class and wanted it to go well. Forgiven?'

Laura cast her a look, mouth firm. 'All right. But you can just tell me things, you know. I am your big sister.' They hugged and packed up in silence. Karen thought, *that's the problem though, you can't just tell her anything. It turns into a big drama.* Still, she was grateful that the tiff had been smoothed over.

Chapter 21

Laura called round to Karen's the day after the class. She arrived with a large bundle in her hands. 'I just wanted to give you something I bought you at the dog show. It's been sitting in my car for ages, and I wasn't sure when to give it to you, but after the successful class, I think you deserve a nice gift,' she hesitated. 'If you don't want it, I can return it. It's for the dogs to lie on, although I'm not sure how it works. It came with impressive testimonies. It's an anti-flea rug. I think that cold you've been hanging on to might be allergies.' She held up her hand to stop Karen whose mouth was open ready to object. 'I know you think your dogs are flea-less, but you could at least try it.'

'Thank you. I know you mean well. They have their anti-flea treatment regularly, but it might help. Thanks sis.'

Laura opened the car door and heaved herself inside. 'I must go now, but we should have a coffee tomorrow and talk about the next class.'

'Sounds good, see you then.' Karen found herself hugging the rug to her chest while she looked around at the dogs panting and smiling at her.

Putting the rug down in the loungeroom, still in its wrapping, Karen went to the door and called the dogs, who came frisking out into the yard. 'Whisky Darling, Spider, Sausage, come on you lot!' She was nearly knocked over and tripped up as they jumped around her. 'Careful, my pretties. Who would feed you if I went to hospital with two broken legs?'

Karen was sweating heavily, and sat for a moment on the garden bench, breathing noisily and wiping her forehead with her sleeve. 'Maybe I'll take some aspirin. What do you think, Sausage?' Sausage had sat heavily on Karen's feet, and she used most of her remaining energy to push the dog off. Treading wearily inside, she threw two aspirin into her mouth and washed them down with a glass of water.

After a cup of tea and a rest in her leather armchair, she felt a little refreshed, and unrolled the parcel Laura had brought her. About two metres long, it was a rich, red mat, edged with black. Rolled inside was a printed page of instructions. It was too much for Karen to absorb in her current fuzzy-headed state, but she read the first paragraph:

FlyAwayFlea™ *is a new product, tested in laboratory conditions in the United States. Not only does FlyAwayFlea*™ *come in a selection of striking colours and designs, but it has proven anti-flea properties. Completely harmless to your pets, FlyAwayFlea*™ *is impregnated with Bioflibonucleicrodemontreme, a chemical which acts immediately on any part of the flea, rendering it incapable of reproducing. No longer will you need to squirt flea control spray onto your furry friends, just let them lie comfortably on the mat and watch their itches disappear.*

Karen sighed and folded up the leaflet to read later. 'Sounds okay. If they don't like it, then they won't lie on it.'

She rolled the mat out and stamped down the edges so they were flat. There was a light, pleasant odour, and she sniffed the air appreciatively. When the dogs came inside, she would see if they went to it of their own accord.

***

Karen spent another restless night, getting up around two o'clock to take some more aspirin, sitting miserably in the kitchen with a cup of tea, waiting for the medicine to take effect. Finally, at about half past three she crept back to bed so as not to disturb Whisky Darling and woke again at six with a throbbing head.

'I'll have to go to the doctor. I wonder if someone could drive me to town,' she posed to Sausage, who wagged her tail and panted some hot saliva onto the hand that was holding a dog biscuit.

Karen wiped the saliva on her jeans, and drifted into the lounge, where Ringo was stretched out on the flea rug that Laura had given her.

'Good boy,' Karen tried to smile, but her mouth wouldn't turn upwards. 'I'm gla-a-a-d you l-l-l-like it. I'll tell Auntie L-L-L-Laura that her gift was a s-s-success.'

She bent down to pat the hound, but a spell of dizziness hit her, and she leant on Ringo for support. He shook himself and moved away, and Karen subsided onto the mat, barely conscious.

'Ringo, come back,' she called, but to no avail. Her chest felt tight, and she struggled to breathe. There was no way she could get up by herself. *I might as well have a nap. At least I know I won't get fleas*, she thought to herself, as consciousness drifted away.

Chapter 22

Laura sat in her loungeroom and bawled her eyes out. Now her own sister was dead, and if she hadn't tried to be kind and buy her a rug, she would still be alive. She thought back over their history. Karen was her only sibling, and, somehow, despite taking a totally different path to Laura, they ended up living in the same country town.

Overwhelmed, reflecting on her life in Cowagulac, she began to despair. 'Look at me,' she sobbed. 'The only man I have ever loved cut his own head off because I frightened him. And to make matters worse, I got bitten by the very spider I thought I could use to win his love. Then Ingrid, of all people, has an outstanding success with Dora's song, and I give our own Jill some beautiful scissors, and then I fall into her with them. And I couldn't save Rosie from being blown over the cliff. Then Dora gets blood poisoning and now look what's happened. My own sister ...' she snorted and gulped as the realisation hit her that, somehow, she had been instrumental in the deaths of so many of her friends. 'I never meant to hurt anyone,' she wailed.

Eventually, her grief wore itself out, and she found herself ravenous. This had been happening more of late, and her appetite had never been small. She recalled the tiff she had with Jill over the mural she had painted, and resolutely turned the mirror away from her so she couldn't see what a whale she had become. 'Jill was right. I should never have interfered with her artistic interpretation.' She felt intensely lonely, not a feeling she was very used to, as there was always something to be organised and arranged.

Pulling open the freezer, she found a container of lasagna, and, while it was defrosting in the microwave, she poured a glass of red wine, sipping it thoughtfully as she looked out the window.

Winter, such as it was, had passed, and the days were getting longer. Karen had loved the long twilights of summer and often called in to Laura's with the dogs after a ramble along the creek. They had shared many glasses of wine accompanied by biscuits and cheese over the years. Karen usually refused a dinner invitation on account of the dogs.

'My God, who's going to look after the dogs?' Laura was appalled that she hadn't thought of this. 'Where are they now? I'd better go and check on them.' Transferring the lasagna from the microwave to the oven took but a moment, then Laura leapt into her car and drove to Karen's. She saw Ingrid's car pulled up outside, and noticed the front door was open. 'Hello?' she called out tentatively, and Ingrid appeared with a medium-sized dog in her arms.

'I thought I'd better stay for a few days and look after them. I hope you don't mind.' She gently placed the dog on the floor, and he sat at her feet, looking up at her adoringly.

'No, no, of course, I am so relieved. I had totally forgotten about the dogs after the drama of the day. I don't know what I'm going to do with them.' Laura peeped uneasily into the loungeroom, and was glad to see the flea rug had been removed.

'I love dogs, so if it's a problem, I will care for them until you make other arrangements. Unless you want them, of course.' Laura hastily shook her head.

'Oh, no, I never understood why Karen loved them so much. I'll arrange for some money to get food for them.'

Ingrid shook her head. 'Not necessary. Karen had all their food arranged in a cupboard, each marked with exactly what the animal should have and there's enough there for about six months, I think, so by then something will have been sorted out.'

Laura patted the bony head by Ingrid's leg. 'I don't mind dogs, I just don't adore them. I guess they will be able to be sold. After all, she was a breeder so they might be worth a bit of money. I'll have to see the solicitor.' Laura sighed. 'So much to arrange.' As she spoke, the memory of the deaths came flooding back and she burst once more into tears.

'There, there. Don't worry about them. I can stay here for a few days, and we can work it out.' But Laura couldn't hear Ingrid for the noisy crying, so Ingrid gave up and went to fetch water and tea. By the time she returned, Laura was calmer but suddenly remembered the lasagna.

'My goodness, are you okay if I leave? I don't want to set my house on fire.'

Luckily, Laura returned to discover that the dish was still edible. So edible in fact that she downed it all, then some ice cream and chocolate sauce. 'Comfort food. I need comforting,' she told herself.

Before long, Laura realised how much she had relied on Karen for companionship. If she had stopped to consider, she might have thought that her relationship was one of big sister to little sister, and that Karen didn't have anywhere near as much to offer Laura as Laura had to offer Karen. But now she came to the realisation that she missed Karen for that very reason. She was one of the few who usually looked up to Laura and admired her. Everyone else seemed to find something to criticise.

In an attempt to develop some replacement friendships, Laura called on Ingrid.

'Hello, anyone home?' Ingrid was out in her lean-to shed but responded to the call.

'Hello to you, Laura. I was just checking the dogs' food for the next week. I thought it was easier to bring it all home, then just go and feed the dogs and walk them twice a day. Have you thought about their future?'

Laura, who was not greedy, nor was she parsimonious, had not. 'Karen has made provision for the dogs' upkeep in her Will, but there's nothing there about what to do if they are sold. I'll have to ask the solicitor whether I have to provide money for the new owner. I do hope not, that would be an enormous task, unless they all go to the same person.'

'I'm glad you came, Laura. there's something I want to discuss with you. Shall we go inside and have a cool drink?' The weather was, as usual, warm. They settled with an ice-cold soft drink, and Laura eyed off the plate of cake and biscuits which Ingrid placed handily within her reach.

'It's very kind of you, Ingrid, to look after the dogs. I would have been hopeless.'

Ingrid tightened her lips and put down her glass. 'Thank you, Laura, I appreciate your kind comment. But that's what I wanted to talk about. You see, I can't keep looking after them. I've decided to move back to town.'

Laura's heart sank. 'But … but you are part of the community here. We can't lose you.' In her head she added, *Not after we have already lost Ned, Rosie, Dora and Karen.*

Ingrid sighed. 'I don't really want to go.'

'Then don't,' Laura interrupted, and Ingrid cast a glance at her that caused her to stop talking.

'I've had a job offer in town. It's all thanks to Velvet's recording. Poor girl. She would have been so happy to know she had made such a hit with that dreadful song.' Noticing Laura's raised eyebrows, she went on 'I can admit that now. It was a shocker, but I couldn't say anything negative about it, not to anyone. But surely you listened to the lyrics. Didn't you think it a bad piece of writing? I shuddered every time I had to hear that dreadful 'but' on the end of the title.'

Laura was shocked. 'I thought … I thought that you thought … and Dora thought …'

Ingrid gave a little laugh. 'Bless her, Velvet didn't think. She really was a simple soul. But I am so glad I won't have to record her anymore. The job I have been offered will give me room to expand to record really talented people. I might even do some singing myself.'

It suddenly struck Laura that Ingrid was not the nice person she had always assumed her to be. Of course, when she was running that course at the CCCC she had been a bit bossy, but then that was to be expected. But now, it didn't seem right to be talking about Dora like that. On the other hand, Laura, if she was honest with herself, agreed with everything Ingrid had said.

'Yes,' she said, drawing the word out so it was more of a drawl. 'I can see your point. Dora was a bit irritating. But I didn't know you felt like that.'

Ingrid drained her glass. 'I make it a habit not to criticise my clients. I wouldn't be successful in this profession if I did that in public. But I don't count you, and I'm sure you understand. After all, there were things about Karen that probably irritated you, too. Sisters can be good friends and equally good enemies.'

Biting and chewing a second piece of cake, Laura thought back to her interactions with her sister. Yes, she could be annoying. But now, she missed her dreadfully. With no other family, she was alone. If she had a child … but no, Laura decided she would not go down that path.

Ingrid stood up. 'I am sorry I can't continue to care for the dogs, but you must understand I have to pack up my place and get it on the market, so I won't be able to spare a couple of hours each day. Is there anyone else you can get to help out?'

Laura thought for a moment. 'I suppose I will have to ask Lancelot. There's no way I could give them the exercise they need. There's too much of me to walk them a couple of kilometres, and there's so many of them.'

'I'll be okay till the weekend but if you could get someone else after that, I'd appreciate it.'

'Is your mind made up, Ingrid? Do you have to leave? Not because of the dogs, of course I'll get them seen to, but I will miss you.'

Ingrid gestured to the frosted jug, but Laura shook her head. 'I'm afraid it's all set. The travel would be too much going to town and back every day, and I think it will be a great career move. I'll miss the village, of course, and everyone.'

Laura stood up to go, and hugged Ingrid. 'I understand. But there won't be much left of Cowagulac before long. To think of all the high hopes I had when we launched that song, and how happy everyone was. And now look at it. Decimated. We do need some people to move into the area.'

'Maybe a couple with eight children will buy my house and double the population at the primary school overnight! I'll ask the estate agent to look favourably on families.'

Laura drove away sadly, resolving to call Lancelot the next day and ask him about the dogs.

The following morning, Laura woke with a dull ache all over her body. 'I wonder if I'm getting the flu.' She turned back the sheet which protected her in some small part from the mosquitoes and swung her legs over the bed. Having a cool shower helped her feel more herself, and she was able to consume some muesli, followed by bacon and eggs. Eventually, she set off for Karen's and saw Ingrid's car was there. Sadness washed over her, but she trod resolutely into the house. Ingrid was measuring out the dry food for the last dog in the row, murmuring to them in loving tones. The dogs were all too busy snuffling into their dishes to care about Laura's appearance. Ingrid stood up and dusted off her knees.

'Hello, Laura. I've fed and walked them this morning, but I am afraid I won't be able to do this anymore. I've just had news that my new apartment is ready, so I have to start moving things today. Will you be able to get Lancelot to help?'

Laura, to her dismay, felt tears prick her eyes. *This is stupid*, she thought, *I'm not that fond of Ingrid. I don't care if she leaves*. But then the thought of all the people who were no longer part of the community hit her, and she staggered to a kitchen chair and sat. Ingrid came over, concerned.

'Are you okay, Laura? You will be able to find someone, won't you? I could come back from Balsham for a couple of days if you need me.'

'No, no, it's fine. I can do it if Lancelot can't and, in any case, they will be sold soon enough. No, you have been a real brick. I can't thank you enough.' She stood and held out her arms. Ingrid hesitated, then joined in a hug. Laura wasn't especially tall, and Ingrid wasn't especially short, but the relative height difference meant that Ingrid's face was jammed into Laura's ample bosom. It wasn't till Ingrid started to struggle that Laura realised she was nearly suffocating her in the embrace. She released Ingrid, who staggered back and sat in the chair.

'My goodness,' she said, gasping for breath. 'You do have a tight old hug.'

'So sorry, Ingrid, it's just that I am going to feel so alone when you go. I only just realised it.'

Ingrid cast her a glance under her lashes that spoke of scepticism, but they parted on friendly enough terms. Several hours later, Laura watched as Ingrid's car, jam packed with boxes and crates, bumped its way down Mermaid Road and out of her life.

***

The next week brought a chat with the solicitor and the swift sale of the dogs via the Breeder's Association. Laura saw them safely into travelling cages with a sigh of relief, tinged with sadness. 'The dogs are *not* Karen,' she told herself firmly. 'Selling them is not like selling my sister.'

And with Karen's house empty, she could then clean it out. The owner, who was charging Laura a nominal rent, was anxious to get it back on the market as soon as possible, so within a matter of days, Karen's presence was all but wiped from the village. Ivy and Geranium had been a constant help to Laura, sorting items and making excursions to drop things off at op shops in Balsham or Fullerton. 'We don't want to be upset by wandering into the Animal Aid shop here in Cowagulac and seeing Karen's jumper in the window, do we?'

Much to Laura's disappointment, there were no hidden treasures, and she ended up keeping only a couple of dog portraits, though she immediately put them facing the wall in her back room.

Chapter 23

Lancelot continued to draw up his list of suspects. *At least Ingrid is safe,* he thought to himself. *Maybe she did the best thing by getting out of here.* It was strange how he didn't stutter when he was thinking to himself.

'It can't be any of the people who are dead. That eliminates quite a few. Who's left?' He pondered this for a while.

I would have accused Rosie. When the solicitor read her Will she showed that that she could be a vindictive old stick. Ivy and Geranium? They're new to the area. What beef could they have against the country folk? Klaus? Hmm, I don't think I've ever heard of a vegetarian murderer. Me? Obviously not. Laura? She's the common factor. But I've known her for years. I can't imagine her doing anything evil. These deaths have been just bad luck. Look at Ned, for example. Even if Laura had planned to kill him, she could hardly have expected he would modify his chainsaw and use it in a plainly dangerous manner. And she did love her sister, I'm sure of that. Of course they argued from time to time – who doesn't? That was the main thing I remember my mother saying – we can choose our friends but not our relatives.

The little voice in the back of his head said, *How many accidents make a murder? Like a parliament of owls, or a quiver of arrows – a wardrobe of murders? A parcel of deaths?*

Lancelot made himself a cup of coffee and had a salad for lunch as he continued to study his spreadsheet. It wasn't very filling, but it came in a handy container from the supermarket. What's more he had got it on special for half price. Lancelot was fond of a good bargain. His mother had been known to make a tasty soup from carrots that had gone limp and bendy. The source of many of his beliefs, she had often said, 'Waste not, want not,' a somewhat mysterious saying which he only understood after he became independent.

He sighed and closed his computer. He had printed out an early copy of the data, but it was lost somewhere on the kitchen table among the papers and bills that really should be put into folders. Anyway, the file was safe enough on his computer.

Without Rosie to help in the radio station, life was very busy. Normally, he would have spoken to Laura about finding a replacement volunteer, but he felt with his unspoken suspicions of guilt that this might be embarrassing, so he chose instead to visit Ivy and Geranium. To tell the truth, he often struggled to remember which was which, having got them confused back at the start when they first came to the community meeting. But he decided to take a chance.

However, as he pulled up at their cottage, he saw Ivy – or at least he thought it was Ivy – in the garden, stooped over, pulling weeds, and adding them to a pile on the ground.

'Hello, there,' Lancelot called out as he closed his car door. 'It's a never-ending task, weeding.'

Ivy stood up and rubbed her back. 'Indeed, you are right. But once I start, I try to keep going till I can see a clear patch. You are just in time for a cup of tea, though. Would you care to come in? I'll see if Geranium can put the kettle on.'

Lancelot accepted, and stood at the door of the kitchen, watching. Both ladies bustled around, seeming to get in each other's way.

'Bless me, dear, watch out for the boiling water.'

'Can I just reach past you and get the packet of biscuits?'

'Have we got any more milk, or shall I fetch some from the other fridge?'

Eventually, the tea was served in an old, china teapot, with a knitted cosy. Matching the teapot were the cups, featuring a hunting scene, and edged with gold. Lancelot considered how annoying the teacups would be, since not only were they small, but you couldn't put them in the microwave or, he assumed, the dishwasher. But if you were truly retired and not busy with volunteering like he was, maybe those little tasks were pleasurable.

'I should have asked you whether you would prefer herbal tea. I have my own mix, which I make from lots of things that grow in our very own garden. It's delicious with a touch of honey.' Geranium looked up with her birdlike expression.

Lancelot thought it sounded nice, but didn't want to stop any longer than he had to, and if they had to repeat their dance manoeuvres to get another pot, he might never get away.

'Thank you, but black tea is fine.'

Small talk over refreshments centred around the recent deaths, and the heightened feelings in the village. The ladies were understandably upset.

'We moved here because it looked such a nice, friendly little place. It's very different from where we were before this. But we have so enjoyed the variety of people and all the activities. And now, with the sad deaths, it seems a different village.' Ivy drained her cup and looked at Geranium. 'And Geranium has been settled here. She often takes a while to get used to a new place, but here it felt like home the moment we found the cottage.'

Lancelot swallowed the last bite of biscuit. 'Where have you lived before this? Do you move around a lot? I had the impression this was a retirement move for you both.'

Geranium began to speak at the same time as Ivy. 'Let me explain to Lancelot. Do you mind?' Ivy spoke firmly and it seemed as though Geranium had no choice. She nodded.

'Geranium lost her husband. We had always been good friends, but, after that, she needed a lot of care and love, as you can imagine. I ended up looking after her, and we decided to get away from the place that had unhappy memories.'

Somehow, it didn't seem appropriate anymore to quiz the ladies about their past, so he reverted to the safe topic of the garden.

'I notice you have been doing such a lot of work in the front garden. It's looking very nice.'

'I'm afraid we ran the water tank dry in the first week we were here. We have had to have a weekly delivery of water. Not something we are used to, but both of us love the garden.' Ivy answered, as Geranium placed the saucers on top of each other and laid the cups carefully on their side.

'I'll just pop these out to the kitchen, unless you want another drink.' Lancelot shook his head and stood up.

'I really should be going anyway. I was doing some complicated work on the computer, but I needed a break and this has been it. Thank you for the tea.'

Ivy walked Lancelot to his car. 'Do forgive Geranium if she seems a little strange sometimes. She went into a deep depression and shock after her husband died suddenly, and even though it's five years ago now, I still worry about her. It's been a godsend moving here. She just loves the village and the country, and as long as I keep her busy, she seems to thrive. And she has your radio station on twenty-four hours a day,' Ivy pressed Lancelot's hand, and fluttered her eyelashes at him.

Suddenly feeling uncomfortable, Lancelot unlocked his car and pulled open the door, finding himself in the awkward position of sitting in the driver's seat but still holding Ivy's hand. He cleared his throat. 'Of course, I understand perfectly.'

Her eyes suddenly downcast, Ivy bent close to Lancelot's face and whispered. 'Please come again. I find it quite lonely here sometimes.'

Releasing his hand, she turned and hurried back up the driveway in response to an imperious summons from Geranium at the front door.

***

That evening, Lancelot spent hours poring over the printout. Even in his sleep, he was muttering and tossing and turning, and woke up in a bath of sweat, feeling no closer to a solution. He started his radio program that day with 'American Pie,' just to give him time to try to click back into some sort of normality, but he found his tongue running away with him when he got to the microphone.

'Bye-bye, indeed. Ladies and gentlemen, that song might well have been written about our dear little village. So many of our residents have said bye-bye, either in a wooden box or departing in their car.' He cleared his throat. 'Let's take a bold look at the deaths. And let us also question whether any one person – or perhaps a group of people – is responsible for them.'

There was a rustle of paper as he laid out his spreadsheet. There followed a remarkable half hour, during which Lancelot fluently outlined a number of theories about the deaths, interspersed with a couple of classical numbers to give himself a breather. Without Rosie in the next office, there was no one to question his broadcast.

Bob came into the studio during a music break. 'You're really giving it to the audience today. I think they'll need my calming animal show – if there's anyone left listening.'

Normally, Lancelot and Bob got on well, but today Lancelot seemed at odds with him. 'Look, Bob, it's got to stop. People are dying all over the place. I put it all in a table, see, here. Oh, hang on, I'll just finish my program, then I'll pop in and see you while the vet does his segment.'

'No vet today, he's called in sick, so I'll be doing the whole show. But let's have a good old chin wag, call round sometime, okay?'

Bob departed to studio two, and Lancelot finished his goodbyes, and stalked out of the radio station.

Chapter 24

As Lancelot left the studio, his mobile vibrated in his pocket. While he was presenting his program, he used to leave the phone with Rosie to answer any incoming calls but now he just put it on vibrate and dealt with any calls later.

He saw Laura's number come up on the screen but just didn't have enough energy to deal with the imperious tone and no doubt a summons. He had given Laura a serve during the program, not exactly blaming her, more implying that she was the string tying the deaths together. As he drove home, the message tone pinged, no doubt to tell him Laura had followed up on her unanswered phone call.

Wearily opening his front door, he dropped his briefcase in the hall and wandered into the kitchen, feeling flat and exhausted. He filled the kettle and switched it on, before shedding his formal radio clothes for some more comfortable garb. It had been a matter of principle that he dressed up for the radio program, even though it wasn't telecast. Barely had the noise of the kettle started when the phone rang again. Sighing, Lancelot answered it with a monotonal, 'Yes, Laura.'

'Lancelot, what do you think you are doing? This is slander. In fact, I think it's libel, I'm sure I read somewhere that radio and TV are libel, not slander. Anyway, you can't go around telling people I murdered half the population.'

'I never said anything of the sort. I was just, well, trying to work it out in my own head.'

There was a moment's silence. Laura sighed heavily. 'I'm feeling a bit sad about it, too. Why don't you come around for a cup of tea and we can talk about it? Just give me an hour to tidy up and pop some biscuits in the oven.'

Although Lancelot was looking forward to relaxing in the recliner chair, he realised that, without Rosie, he had very few people to chat with, so he accepted Laura's invitation. Pulling the recliner footrest up, he pushed aside the odd interaction with Ivy when she stuck her head in his car. *Lonely old lady,* he thought. He started looking again at his spreadsheet, then remembered with a start that he was on radio shift again the next morning, so instead started trawling through some newspapers on the net for material to present.

He usually found some snippets of quirky things in country newspapers from surrounding areas. A mouse plague had given him material for several shows, with some great audio of squealing people trying to rid their houses of invasions, and on another occasion, a shark nearly snatching a paddle boarder led to some great interviews with witnesses. He didn't let it bother him that about one percent of the Cowagulac population would have even seen the surf, let alone ridden a wave.

The visit to Ivy and Geranium popped up in his mind. *Where* did *they come from?* he wondered, and without hesitation typed 'Ivy Vine Geranium Golightly' into the search bar. Nothing came up, so he tried them individually. Golightly, being an unusual name, gave him a few leads, and he came across the death notice for the man he presumed was her husband. *How sad*, he thought, as he read the obituary for Henry Golightly. 'Suddenly, at home,' was the descriptor used for his death. What would it be like to find your partner dead in your own house? Was it in bed? Perhaps a heart attack? He looked up the coroner's report.

Toxicological analysis of pre-mortem samples identified the presence of alcohol at a concentration level of 0.16g/100mL. Similar analysis of post-mortem samples detected the presence of therapeutic drugs.

'Hmm, I wonder what therapeutic drugs were found. What a pity it doesn't go into more detail.' Lancelot continued perusing the document.

Having considered all the available evidence, I am satisfied that no further investigation is required in this case. I convey my sincere condolences to the family for their loss.

Lancelot thought back to the conversation with Ivy. 'Five years ago. Tough call, if you've been married for decades.'

Just about to close the computer and go to Laura's he swiped his finger down the other internet searches for Golightly and Vine. Perhaps Ivy had been married, too. Divorced? Widowed? Or never married? She seemed a nice old stick, and very helpful to Geranium. They had certainly been an asset to Cowagulac.

Nothing more came up for Golightly, and there was so much on Vine, mostly to do with gardening, that he closed the computer and headed for Laura's.

Chapter 25

The discussion went better than Lancelot had expected. Laura seemed calm and reasonably objective about the radio broadcast.

'I quite understand how upset you are. After all, Lancelot, in many ways, you are the glue that binds this village together. We all listen to the local station, and I don't think any of us feel happy about how things have changed in a matter of a year. Sure, the country wasn't zooming ahead with development and business, but we had just got the CCCC and the high hopes we had around that making us the hub of the area and even stealing the title of the biggest town from Balsham … all those hopes are so far away now.'

The smell of biscuits baking was making Lancelot's mouth water. 'How happy we were. Though that first meeting at the CCCC when everyone was making such a fuss wasn't so much fun. But we were a real community. Now who do we have left? How do we replace the fussiness of Rosie, the quirkiness of Ned …' Lancelot stopped short as he realised that both Laura's sister and her potential boyfriend had died.

'Anyway,' he went on hastily, 'the question is whether they were all accidents, or whether we have some evil lurking here in our town.'

The timer on the oven alerted Laura that the baking was done, and she excused herself to make tea. 'Black, Lancelot?'

'Yes, or herbal tea if you have some. Otherwise, just plain, weak black, thank you.' Lancelot had learned over the years to keep his order simple. Asking for 'just a dash of low-fat milk,' had often ended up with half a cup of cream floating on the top.

The conversation, which Lancelot had dreaded being acrimonious, turned into a very pleasant event. As he was leaving, Laura suddenly stopped. 'Wait, I have something for you.' She ran to the kitchen and returned with a small cellophane wrapped packet of dried herbs. 'Would you like this? It was a gift to me, but I hate herbal tea. It might be something you would like, though. If not, just pop it in the compost bin.'

Lancelot was touched. 'Thank you, Laura, that's very kind of you. I usually have peppermint tea to help me sleep, so perhaps I will try this tonight, instead.'

He sighed as he drove away. He had never been conscious of feeling lonely, but perhaps he had been without realising it. Of course, Laura was far too young to be considered for a partner, but maybe a closer friendship would be possible.

He decided on a later dinner, since he had eaten several of the still-warm biscuits baked by Laura, and was feeling slightly uncomfortable in the tummy. Opening his computer again, he scanned the 'Ivy Vine' entries. While there were many still directly involved with gardening – he did wonder which parent or unfortunate marriage had combined *Ivy* with *Vine* – and tracked down an article from the *Western Plains News*. Opening the entry, he found a photo of the mayor of Ivy and Geranium's previous town. The man was impressively decorated with a gold chain and robes, under the heading, 'Mourners celebrate the life of Mayor Frelling.'

Curious as to how Ivy's name appeared in such an article, he read on.

Mayor Frelling died following a fall from the steps of council chambers last week. He was leading a tour of the chambers to a group of distinguished citizens, who had been invited to a morning tea with the council. Posing at the top of the steps, he appeared to lose his footing and fall, to the horror of the group as the photographers at the bottom of the staircase. (See inset picture). Ivy Vine, Mayoral secretary, thanked everyone for their condolences.

Using a magnifying glass, Lancelot examined the smaller photo. Sitting back in his chair, he blinked several times, then used his mobile to take a photo of the article, enabling him to zoom in to get a grainy, but larger, image. 'No. I don't believe it.'

Chapter 26

Klaus was now confident that he could travel astrally without too much fear of eternal wandering in the ether. He lay on the couch, closed his eyes and clutched his crystal, which had chipped slightly when it fell from his chest last time, but he didn't think that would matter much. Between last session and this one, he had done a bit more reading, so knew what to do. He had blessed the room to prevent devils entering, but he figured that since he didn't believe in either devils or prayer, they would cancel each other out. He had sorted through his phone contacts to see if anyone needed healing since it was said that he could pour the light into a sick person and make them well. Fortunately, no one he knew of was suffering with an illness. Besides, he was meant to feel only love for whoever he was intending to heal, and Klaus conceded that the main person in the world he loved was himself.

He was asleep within moments, or at least off wandering in space somewhere. This time, he felt the vibrations. His teeth chattered and his arms were shaking, but he couldn't control them. It was not a comfortable feeling, but, soon, things became calmer, and he found himself outside in familiar pastures, just near Ned's shed. Passing through the wall of the shed with a swimming motion, he was able to see the empty shelves, where the chainsaws had been stored, and idly wondered where they had all gone. There was a half sawn sculpture in the corner, and he lingered there, trying to work out what it was, but gave up when he remembered how interpretive Ned's work was. Some small machinery pieces were still on shelves and hanging from hooks, but he couldn't recognise any of them.

He enjoyed the sensation of spinning round and pictured his life cord winding around and around him like a cocoon. He floated over the site of the UFO landings. *How ironical,* he thought, *if they landed and I saw them, but they couldn't see me.* There was silence, and although Klaus searched the skies there was nothing to be seen. Onward he went, over the field of wheat which was in a burst of near summer growth.

Suddenly it all made sense. The crop circles, the careful design, appearing overnight, convincing him that aliens were landing. The solution came to him. 'Of course, when astral travelling you will see things that the normal human does not, and have experiences no one can believe.' He had read this, and now, now he believed it. To his surprise, he was able to push off from a tree and headed back to Ned's shed, and inspected the few machines left hanging on the wall more closely. A laser cutter. And right next door, a drone. Blast and curse Ned! Though one should not think ill of the dead, Ned had set him up. Laser cutting using the drone. Klaus was sure there would be a way of programming the damn thing so it cut the right patterns. He always thought there was something not quite genuine about Ned, even though he pulled the wool over the eyes of most people. He should have offered a class at the CCCC in the art of deception, for surely no one would want to attend one on tree stump carving. But what did this laser machine mean? Were all his UFO experiences false? Or just the ones where Ned was playing a prank on him? Surely it was just the crop circle. That could have been done easily enough, now he thought about it. But how could Ned have managed the lights? Drone technology could do anything these days. No! Klaus thought back to Rosie and what her parents had reported.

Despite Ned's evil sense of humour, playing such a trick on him, he still believed in the mystery of the space craft he had never actually seen.

The white light which had accompanied Klaus since he started his journey weakened, and he immediately made sure to think to pleasant thoughts. He might lose protection if he thought negatively.

'How clever of Ned,' he hastily revised his wording. 'I wish he had let me in on the secret. Perhaps we could have had fun with more unsuspecting people.'

Now he felt weaker and lacking in energy, so thought himself back to his loungeroom. Lingering for a moment, he watched his peaceful body lying there, twitching slightly, before he melted back inside it, and drifted into a long sleep.

Waking up in the middle of the night, Klaus felt refreshed and ravenous. The last time he had travelled, he made sure to fill his belly, but this time, his eagerness to travel had overtaken his normal dinnertime. Without bothering to check the clock, he walked, somewhat wobbly still, to the kitchen, where he searched the fridge for anything edible. A woven basket filled with mushrooms met his eye, and he immediately set the frying pan on low while he washed and sliced the entire contents of the basket. He couldn't recall where they had come from, and they were not his own, but nevertheless, they were all the button variety, which suited his numerology requirement to perfection.

The knife flashed as it sliced, and every so often he popped a segment in his mouth. Scraping the mushrooms off the board and into the pan led to a satisfactory sizzling in the hot butter. A sprinkle of salt was all they needed to make a dish fit for kings.

The grandfather clock in the hall chimed three sonorous notes, and he thought for a moment about whether having a meal at that time was good for his digestion, but after all, you couldn't go wrong with mushrooms, and he felt ready to start the day anyway.

Sitting at the table, he tucked a serviette into his shirt and settled down with his plate. It was his habit to eat quite slowly and enjoy the sensations of heat and flavour as the food hit the tastebuds. The first forkful, he allowed to sit on his tongue, while the juices slid slowly down his throat. He pictured the button tops growing in the ground, emerging as tiny pinheads and developing into fully flavoured fungus, then being picked gently by hand ready for preserving or cooking. A deep sigh escaped as he chewed and swallowed.

His mind wandered to the astral experience he had just had. Poor Ned. What a character he had been. After his travelling session, he felt sad and rather than angry about Ned's actions. Someone so determined to pay back Klaus for whatever imagined slight that he had gone to the trouble of laser cutting a crop circle. If only Ned had used his talents for good. Why, a bit of publicity in the right places and Cowagulac could have become a tourist mecca. People would have flocked in, money in the tills of coffee shops and the CCCC. The council could have lowered rates instead of raising them each year. But now Ned was dead. Not only him, but Rosie, Karen, Dora and Jill.

Suddenly his throat swelled. *Five! Five people dead*, he thought. Klaus coughed and tried to dislodge a piece of mushroom that had gone the wrong way down his throat. But he became fixated on the deaths. Five, not an even number. There must be one more. That would be divisible by two. He coughed again, and, as he coughed, his throat swelled more and more. He gasped for breath and heard only a whistling sound escape, as oxygen became harder and harder to get. In his final moments, Klaus could think only one thing. His death would make the numbers even. All was right with the world.

Chapter 27

Lancelot washed the dinner dishes and decided on a night of television. Putting the kettle on, he scooped some tea from Laura's gift into the warmed pot and waited while the kettle boiled. 'What rubbish is there to watch? Hmm, celebrity this and celebrity that. I wonder what qualifies you as a celebrity. I've got a Bachelor of Arts and a Grad Dip in journalism. What would they have? A Certificate II in Self-Promotion? Maybe a Diploma of Idiocy? This could be a good editorial for the show tomorrow. Unless people actually like these shows.' He sighed and pushed himself up out of the chair. 'I might put a whole lot of my audience offside if they get insulted.'

The hiss of water on the leaves and the aroma that arose helped him relax, and he dropped his tense shoulders and swirled the pot around before he strained it into a fine bone china mug. Accustomed to talking to himself, he questioned whether he should put sugar, or a little honey in the drink, but decided to wait and see how it tasted.

Once more in the big leather chair, he settled on watching a quiz show, and took a tentative sip of the tea. 'Ah, that's good. No need for sweeteners.' The show was mildly amusing, and when it was over, he started looking over his research on Ivy and Geranium.

'So, Ivy was a secretary to the mayor. I wonder if she found that hard to give up when they moved. But ...' He picked up the magnifying glass from the table next to the chair and squinted at the photo on the screen. 'I'm nearly one hundred percent certain that is Geranium. What would she have been doing in the photo?' He sat back and let the computer rest on his lap. 'Geranium is standing right behind the mayor. Maybe she also worked there.'

Rather than type with the computer balanced on his knee, he jotted down some thoughts in a small notebook.

Geranium in photo? Mayor dies. Ivy present at function. No further action.

Geranium's husband dies of toxic substance. Ivy close friend. No further action.

Ivy and Geranium move to Cowagulac for no real reason. Ivy decided on location.

In casual conversation, Ivy mentioned Geranium's household help had been run over. Investigate to find further details.

Check coroner report on mayor. Interview people who were there.

Satisfied with the investigatory steps he could take the next day, Lancelot laid back in the chair and found himself slipping into sleep. Remembering the stiff neck he woke with last time he had fallen asleep in the chair, he forced himself awake enough to transfer himself to bed.

***

Bob Suttie climbed into his car to head to the radio station, early, as usual, to prepare for his show. Switching on to CowRadio, he was surprised to hear static. Pressing a few buttons randomly, he expected to get reception, but the silence continued. Vaguely disturbed by this, Bob accelerated to town, only to find the CowRadio building still locked. By now considerably worried, he called Lancelot. When he got no answer, he rang Laura.

'What's happening, Laura? The station is locked, and I can't get any reception on the radio. Where's Lancelot?'

'I don't know, I was just about to head over to his place. It's very unlike Lancelot not to be there, or to let anyone know if he couldn't make it. I don't recall him ever missing a program, but maybe he's sick, or had an accident. Shall I meet you there?'

'I think I'd better go in to check and get the program up and running. People will be wondering what's going on. Maybe call the police. Without Rosie, no one is around to help the presenters anymore, so I'll have to produce my own show.'

'Okay, I'll let you know what happens.'

Laura called Constable Makepeace as she drove to Lancelot's. 'Can you come over? I've got a feeling something is wrong. I only saw Lancelot yesterday and he was fine, but he never misses his radio time.'

'Wait till I get there, okay?'

'But I'll be there in a minute. What if he's had a heart attack and needs help? Every minute might be important.'

'I'll put the blues and twos on and be there in five minutes, okay?'

As it happened, Laura pulled up at almost the same time that the police car screeched around the corner. Lancelot's house was fairly secluded, and Makepeace told Laura to stay put while he checked the entrance.

'We don't know what might have happened. I don't want you put in any danger.' His face reddened slightly, and he hastily continued. 'That is, no members of the public should be put in danger.'

Once he gave the all-clear, they banged on the door and shouted, before the constable used his elbow to smash the small window in the front door and open the latch. Making Laura stay behind him, he called out as he explored each room. 'Lancelot, it's the police. Are you there?'

They arrived at the bedroom, and Laura caught a glimpse before Makepeace closed the door and told her to wait in the kitchen. 'Don't touch anything. Just wait.'

He called his sergeant, who set things in train back at the station, then returned to the room. Lancelot was lying half in, half out of the bed, back arched, face in a grimace that exposed his false teeth plate, which had come loose. The beside lamp was on the floor, the mobile phone pulled out of the charger, and the computer in two halves at the foot of the bed. The fine bone china mug was in pieces halfway across the room.

Meanwhile, Laura was on the phone to Bob, telling him the reason Lancelot had not been there. 'But, don't say anything on the radio, not until we get the all-clear from the police.'

Laura looked around the kitchen and saw the teapot and bag of tea she had given him. She half rose to clear the mess, until she recalled Makepeace's firm instruction not to touch anything and subsided back into the chair. She felt numb. Another death.

It wasn't long before the ambulance and senior police officers arrived, and Laura saw the flash of photos being taken and heard the murmur of voices. Some time later, a stretcher carried Lancelot's body out of the house, covered decorously with a white sheet. 'I'm glad it's not a body bag like the movies,' said Laura to Makepeace, who had come into to the kitchen.

'We have a preliminary cause of death. Looks like he ingested poison of some sort.' The policeman was pale and a little sweaty. He hadn't expected his quiet country posting to involve quite so many bodies as it had the last year. 'What was his mental state, Laura? Do you know?'

Laura pursed her lips. 'Not suicidal, if that's what you are asking. Like all of us, he was distressed about the deaths in Cowagulac, and he had broadcast all his thoughts only … was it yesterday? Then he came to see me, because he said some nasty things about …' Laura bit her lip, suddenly realising she was possibly giving herself a motive.

'About whom, or about what?' Makepeace might not have had a reputation as a great academic, but he had sound common sense.

Laura gulped. 'Well, about me, actually. But he came around to my place and we talked about it.'

'Was anyone else there?' A notebook had appeared in Makepeace's hand, and he was writing down the conversation.

'No, just me and him. I rang him at the radio station. You can probably check the call records. And he apologised and I asked him round for a cup of tea. He came, he ate, he drank, we talked, and it was all good.'

Makepeace's tongue was sticking out of the corner of his mouth as he tried to capture every word. Finally, he closed the notebook and said 'Well, Laura, I expect the sarge will want you to make a statement at the station. But tomorrow will be fine for that.'

Pulling some plastic gloves out from a little container on his belt, the constable put them on. 'I'm going to check the kitchen now. You better leave, or the sarge will want to know why you are still here.'

Laura felt vaguely disturbed as she drove away and was happy to see Geranium and Ivy walking along the main street. She tooted her horn and the ladies looked around in surprise.

'Ahoy, how are you? Have you time for coffee?' Laura called out. Ivy came over to the car and rested her arms on the open window.

'Of course, there's always time for coffee. You'd better park the car, though, before someone runs into the back of you.'

'Meet you in Chatter 'n' Natter.'

Ivy and Geranium were already seated by the time Laura arrived.

'I've put in an order for a latte and some muffins, dear, I think you said you liked the double chocolate ones?' Ivy patted the seat next to her.

'Oh, thank you. I was going to try and avoid them, but since they are on the way, I'll start that diet tomorrow.'

'You don't need to diet!' Geranium, who was stick thin, always supported plumper people to feel okay about their weight. 'You're a comfortable weight, I'm sure.'

'Thank you, Geranium. I've always enjoyed my food. Here they come now.'

The café had a great reputation for their fine muffins, and these oozed melted chocolate inside, so were always served slightly warm, with cream on the side. Ivy and Laura tucked in, with Geranium looking on, nodding approvingly. 'Have a little more cream, dear. It's a natural product, and I believe dairy is now meant to be good for you. It's so confusing, one year, eggs are evil, then next they are a health saviour. But dairy is always good.'

Laura hastily swallowed, suddenly reminded of the events of the morning. 'I have some news for you. Not good, either. Poor Lancelot, he's dead. I found his body.'

'No!' Ivy had gone pale. Geranium continued sipping her coffee, looking around with wide eyes over the top of her cup. 'What happened?' Ivy lowered her voice when she saw people looking at them. 'Did he have a fall?'

'Much worse than that. The police think he ingested poison.'

Both ladies muttered exclamations, cut short by Laura's continuing commentary. 'He didn't turn up for his program this morning, and Bob Suttie rang me about it. I went round, and Makepeace was with me. We found his body. It was awful. But I'm not meant to say anything yet, so keep it between us, okay?'

'Of course, my dear, neither Geranium nor I would say anything to a soul. How awful.'

***

Laura fielded five phone calls that evening, so it became quickly apparent that either Ivy or Geranium was not able to keep a secret. Laura doubted it would have been the police who released the information.

In response to a call from Makepeace, Laura attended the police station the following day. Once she had finished making her statement, she gathered her bag and was about to leave when the sergeant appeared at the door.

'Would you mind waiting a moment? There's a couple more things to clear up.'

'Sure,' Laura paused, and the sergeant buzzed her through to a small interview room. Makepeace joined them, nodding to Laura.

'Please be seated.' The sergeant reappeared in the room, holding a package with three DVDs tightly wrapped in plastic and a thick manilla folder, as well as a dark blue leather-bound diary. 'We will be recording this interview, Laura, so at the end you will receive one of these DVDs.'

'What am I meant to do with it?' Laura started to get hot and cold, somehow at the same time, and an ominous feeling took hold of her stomach.

'Let me get these started, and I will explain it to you.'

The sergeant took the seat next to the machine which had been wheeled in on a trolley, while Makepeace sat directly opposite Laura. After some digestive whirls and clicks, a video picture of Laura appeared on a tiny screen, and she grimaced. 'Oh, I don't want to see that. I look horrible!'

Makepeace nodded. 'It's a bit like your driver's licence photo. But don't worry, it goes off a few seconds after the interview starts.'

Sergeant Inglis put a small black disc in front of Laura, and explained it was the microphone. 'Just speak clearly, if you would.'

Laura half rose, wanting to leave, but a tiny shake of the head from Makepeace saw her slide back into the chair.

'This is a recorded interview between Laura Adams and Sergeant Inglis. Also present is my corroborator ...'

'Constable Makepeace.'

'Laura, you are not under arrest and are free to leave at any time. Do you understand?'

Laura nodded, but the sergeant said, 'Please speak for the recording.'

'Oh, of course, yes, I understand.'

'Although you are not under arrest, I will explain your rights. You have the right to remain silent, you have the right to communicate with or attempt to communicate with a friend or relative to inform them of your whereabouts, you have the right to communicate with or attempt to communicate with a legal practitioner. If you are not a citizen or permanent resident of Australia, you have the right to contact the consular office of the country of which you are a citizen. Do you understand these rights?'

Laura felt like crying, but told herself they hadn't arrested her, and she was able to leave, she reminded herself.

Almost as though she was observing herself, she was a little intrigued in the police process. If only it hadn't been her in the hot seat.

'Yes,' she said. 'I understand'

'And do you wish to exercise any of these rights?'

Laura almost laughed at the thought of her doing any exercise, until she caught the sergeant's eye and shook her head. 'No.'

'Very well. I have asked you to do this interview because we are investigating the death of Lancelot Charger. Could you please tell us how you came to be at Lancelot's house and discovered his body?'

'I've just said all that in the statement. Do I have to go through it again?'

'Please.'

Laura sighed heavily. 'Lancelot didn't come on CowRadio for his usual program timeslot. I didn't think anything of it except that it must have been bad reception, but Bob Suttie, who has the program after Lancelot, rang me and said the station was all locked up. I thought that sounded odd and told him to meet me at Lance's house. But Bob thought he should start his own program, so I called Constable Makepeace. Bob thought people would be wondering why the station was off the air.'

'And what happened when you arrived at the house?'

'The constable broke in, and we found the body.'

'And then?'

'He sent me to wait in the kitchen.'

'Did you touch anything?'

'No, I had been told not to.'

'Do you go often to Lancelot's house?'

'No, hardly ever. He was a bit of a fusspot, a recluse, and didn't ask people over. But he was okay about coming to visit other people.'

'Can you explain why we found your fingerprints in the kitchen?'

Laura looked puzzled. 'Not especially. I mean, I haven't been there for ages. Why?'

The sergeant ignored the question. 'What can you tell me about a bag of tea?'

'Tea? What sort of tea?'

'A plastic bag, ziplock, with dried tea leaves in it.' He opened the manila folder and took out a photo. 'This is the bag I am talking about.'

'Oh. Yes, I gave that bag to Lance yesterday. He came over to talk about what he had said on the radio program. I wasn't very happy about some of his comments. But we sorted it all out.'

'Why did you give him a bag of tea?'

Laura went red. 'Well, to tell the truth, it was a gift to me, but I hate herbal tea, and Lancelot likes it, so I thought, rather than waste it, I'd hand it on. I didn't tell him where it came from. I just told him it was a gift.'

'And where did you get it from?'

'It was a present from Geranium Golightly. She dries the herbs herself, but I had some once and it was horrible. Now, if she makes me a cup, I just accept it and pour it into a pot plant.'

The sergeant and constable exchanged glances. Laura, who had started to feel comfortable, felt her heart skip a beat.

'When did you get this bag of tea?'

'Oh, only a few days ago. Geranium always said it was best when fresh. She told me to put it in an airtight container, but I didn't get around to it.'

There was a pause. 'Anything you want to ask, senior?'

The sergeant looked at Makepeace, who pursed his lips, then replied, 'Not at this time sarge.'

The sergeant continued, 'You are telling me, Laura, that you got a bag of tea from Miss Golightly, handed it on to Lance, and that's all you know about it? You didn't open the bag?'

'Not that I recall. It always had that slightly seaweedy, mildewy smell which was not very pleasant.'

'And you are sure you didn't open the bag, at all?'

'I'm sure.'

'Very well, I think that's all for now. Interview concluded at eleven twenty-five AM.'

Laura let out a big sigh and realised she had barely been breathing for the last half hour. 'What happens now?'

'Our investigations will continue.' He pulled each of the DVDs out and put them in plastic covers, then clicked the lids shut. 'Here's your copy. I would appreciate it if you didn't discuss this with anyone for a few days. Constable Makepeace will show you out.'

The fresh air smelled good after the stuffy interview room, and Laura stood on the steps of the police station for several minutes, allowing herself to calm down, trying to work out what had just happened. If only she could talk things over with Karen. Annoying she might have been, but once you got her to concentrate, she was pretty full of common sense.

Just as she descended the steps, the door was pushed open, and Makepeace appeared. 'Laura! I'm glad to catch you. Do you know who Lancelot's solicitor was?'

'No idea, I'm afraid. Have you found anything in his papers?'

'Not at his home. I wondered if he kept anything at the radio station.'

'I doubt that. Do you want me to check? I can go there now.'

'I'll come with you. Or rather, I'll follow you in the car. Is that okay?'

'Sure. I'd rather not ride in a police car if it's all the same to you.'

While they were searching the various shelves and cupboards in the station, Laura quizzed the policeman. 'What was that all about today? I gather my fingerprints were on the bag of tea. But how did you get my fingerprints to match them?'

'Don't you remember? We asked for them after Karen died.'

Laura nodded. 'Oh, yes. Did you find any other prints on the bag?'

'Lancelot's, and there was one unknown partial print. But with your help, we think it may have been Geranium's.'

'That would make sense. Do you know what the poison was yet?'

'It seems like it was hemlock, but we have to wait for the toxicology people to do the tests. The symptoms Lance showed are consistent with hemlock. The symptoms don't come on suddenly, they can take a few hours.'

'Do you think it was in the tea?'

'Might have been. Don't know yet what else he ate or drank.'

'But if it was in the tea, I might have drunk some and died. Ew!' Laura was horrified but Makepeace seemed unaffected by the thought of her sudden demise.

'Well, there's no paperwork here. I'll go back to Lancelot's and have another squiz. Coming?'

'Sure. Maybe I'll join the police force as a new career.'

'Just don't touch anything and don't tell the sarge.'

The police security tape had been removed from Lancelot's house, and Makepeace had the front door key. The window he broke had been taped up. Laura shuddered as she went in, recalling the scene from yesterday. 'I think I might just sit and wait for you,' she said.

'Okay, wait in the lounge. That's been thoroughly searched.'

Laura thought about a cup of tea, but, recalling the information from the interview, decided she could wait. She sat in the lounge chair and pulled the lever that allowed the footrest to slide into position. It was very comfortable. *I'd like one of these for myself, I wonder how much it cost.* Laura leaned back, but there was something uncomfortable under her hip. She wiggled around and extracted a small notebook, with a heavy cardboard cover. Sounds of drawers being pulled open and closed could be heard from upstairs, so she opened the book. Staring back at her were Lancelot's notes, which cast quite the unflattering light onto Ivy and Geranium.

Eager for more, Laura flicked the page over, to read *Milk, bread, eggs, cottage cheese*.

Hearing the constable's boots clumping down the stairs Laura was left with a rapid decision to make. She was under suspicion, and this notebook might exonerate her. But on the other hand, she would like to investigate it herself. Quickly activating her phone, she took a photo of the earlier page, then called out. 'Makepeace, I found this in the chair!'

The constable was very excited at the discovery and wanted to hasten back to the police station. He took the book in both hands and felt the warmth of Laura's fingers as she released it. They were both eager to get away and start some research, so they exited and went their separate ways.

Stopping only for a warmed-up pizza, several rice balls, a packet of chips, and some chocolate gateau from the freezer, Laura searched the internet. Such a wealth of information to be found, once you had a few details. By midnight, Laura felt she had some answers and sat back in her chair. It was going to be a long night, because she didn't think she would be able to sleep. The question was, what should she do with the information? Just tamely hand it over to the police, or should she confirm a few of the details?

She woke in the morning, stiff and sore from having fallen asleep in the chair. But her mind was clear. A shower, breakfast, and another look at what she had found, as well as the list of questions she had drafted, and she felt ready.

Driving to Ivy and Geranium's house, she was excited and a little scared. Not of the two women, because, after all, they were old, and she was confident that she could handle both of them if it came to the crunch. She set her mobile to voice record as she knocked at the door.

Geranium answered with her pleasant smile, 'Come in my dear, I was expecting you.'

Laura hesitated but stepped over the threshold. 'Why were you expecting me?'

'I heard you were at the police station yesterday. Nothing much stays secret in this village. I guess you know that my tea was responsible for dear Lancelot's death. I'm so sad about that. I was convinced you would drink it. I wished no harm to Lancelot.'

Laura felt the situation was rapidly getting out of her control. 'The police didn't say anything about that. They just asked me about my fingerprints on the bag.'

'Tut, tut dear. Don't think you can fool me.' There was a hard edge to her voice which Laura had not heard before. Geranium patted the couch. 'Come and sit down and tell me what you have found out.'

Laura wanted to run away, but there was something hypnotic and compelling about the old woman's eyes.

Obediently, she sat down. 'Where's Ivy?'

'Just running some errands, dear. And what do you have in your handbag? I see there are some papers sticking out. You might as well tell me, though I daresay it won't be a surprise.'

Laura took a deep breath. Nothing to lose, she thought. 'Very well. Lancelot had made some notes, and I have followed them up. Your husband died of an unidentified toxic substance. The Mayor of Parlington died when he fell down some stairs, and you were standing right behind him at the time. Your housekeeper was run over by a vehicle that was very similar to the one you and Ivy drove. I think you killed those people.'

Laura waited for a reaction from the old lady who was sitting opposite her. There was nothing more than a raised eyebrow. 'And your proof? If this is true, I should tell you, the police in two other towns have never even questioned me, let alone arrested me. Which is more than I can say for you, dear.'

Laura opened her bag and pulled out the photo and printouts from her internet searches. 'Here you are. I think the police will be very interested in such a lot of coincidences.'

'Perhaps they will be. By the way, would you like a cup of tea? I promise you can open the container yourself. And there are some fresh cookies Ivy baked this morning.' Laura was feeling a little peckish but even she drew the line at hospitality with a possible murderer.

'No thank you. I just wondered what you had to say before I handed this over to the police.'

'My dear, I am sorry you think I am such an evil person. By all means, go to the police with your pathetic little story. I am sure it will divert them away from the truth.'

'And what is the truth?' Laura started to feel uncertain, losing confidence in the face of Geranium's calm assuredness.

'If you care to come with me, I can show you the truth.' Laura hesitated. 'Come, come. You have nothing to fear from me, I assure you.'

Geranium led the way to the kitchen, and opened the door, then stood aside. 'Here's your murderer, I'm very sad to say. I've protected Ivy all these years but finally her madness got so out of hand I couldn't control her any longer. It was for her own good, and the good of the village.'

Ivy lay on the kitchen floor, a pool of blood still seeping along the cracks in the tiles. 'She came at me this morning, when I said I thought it was all over. I only hit her with the mallet, but she must have fallen and hit her head. So sad.'

Laura ventured forward to check for a pulse, and as she did so, Geranium lunged at her, having picked up the blood-stained mallet. It struck a glancing blow, but only on Laura's shoulder. She cried out, trying to run towards the back door.

'Oh no, my dear, you must join Ivy. I can't let you go now.' With a remarkable burst of speed, the older woman almost caught up with Laura as she staggered and slipped in the blood. 'Help, help! Can anyone hear me?' Laura pulled in desperation at the back door, but was flung across the room when it burst open and the large frame of Constable Makepeace appeared in the doorway.

Makepeace took a firm hold of Geranium's arm, which still held the mallet, forcing her to drop it. Given his size compared to the bird like lady, he was able to hold both her wrists in one of his huge hands, fishing out his handcuffs with the other. Geranium was spitting and snarling, muttering incomprehensible curses at the policeman and Laura, but it wasn't long before she was secured. The fight suddenly went out of her, and she drooped over the table, though Laura was suspicious that this was just an act and at any moment she might kick off again. However, Makepeace got through the caution – 'Now Ms Golightly, you do not have to say or do anything, but anything you say or do may be used in evidence. Do you understand?' – and handed the old lady over to his relief officers, merely saying, 'Don't trust her. She might be old but she's crafty.' At that Geranium let out a cackle and allowed herself to be taken off in a police car.

An ambulance attended Laura and declared her fit to carry on. She sat unmoving and stunned in a kitchen chair, which was the only one the police allowed her to use. She watched, eyes glazed, as Ivy's body was photographed and removed. An immense sadness washed over her and she felt angry that she had not seen there was something wrong with Geranium sooner. Instead, she had spread the story to them about Lancelot, when obviously Geranium already knew all about it.

Chapter 28

It was a sad group of Cowagulac residents who made their way to Balsham for the preliminary hearing against Geranium. She had been charged with just one murder, that of Ivy, though Makepeace had promised that more charges would follow. First of all, the police had to establish whether Geranium was of sufficiently sound mind to stand trial. This would be determined at the coronial inquest at the Balsham Magistrates' Court.

'Magnum,' Laura had come to be on first name terms with the constable after she presented her phone recording of Geranium's admission. She was now more understanding of why Makepeace never revealed his first name, preferring to go only by his rank. Laura, in her usual tactless way, asked if he was named after an ice cream, and somewhat shamefacedly, he had told her that, indeed, his parents had made love after eating the delicacy, and consequently chose that for his first name.

'Magnum, you have enough evidence to charge her with Lancelot's murder. She admitted it on the phone recording.'

'True, Laura, but my boss said to establish whether she is of sound mind or not first. It's not going to make much difference whether it's one, two or a whole lot of murders, really. Any sentence she gets would be enough to see her out for her natural life. We don't do that American thing of adding fifteen life sentences on top of each other.' Laura was a bit disgruntled but had enough on her plate with the potential of being called as a witness.

The little courtroom was full a good half hour before the hearing began. Most of the remaining residents were there, the mayor and her husband, a group of reporters from the nationals as well as the local paper, and there were TV cameras out the front, as well as a helicopter covering overhead. The locals made sure that there was no room for the pesky politician who made his appearance five minutes before court was due to start. Handbags and jackets were spread on seats, and heads studiously turned to avoid looking at James Thurber, MP. Eventually, he gave up and left. A quiet smatter of applause followed his exit.

Laura had a microphone shoved in her face and uttered a quiet, 'No comment,' as she went up the steps of the courthouse. She knew she might be called to give evidence that morning and had dressed carefully in a dark jacket and nearly matching pants.

However, once the court had been called to order and the magistrate had opened proceedings, the barrister appearing for the prosecution, rose.

'Your Worship, you will note Ms Golightly is not in court. I should explain to Your Worship that she is currently undergoing assessment and treatment in a psychiatric hospital. I have several reports from her treating doctors and psychiatrists which I would like to tender to the court.'

At a nod from the magistrate, the clerk handed over the documents, which the magistrate read slowly and laboriously, following some of the text with a finger. The lawyer was standing by the lectern, switching from foot to foot as the pages were slowly turned over. At last, he finished. 'Thank you, Mr Swayfield. It appears to me that the medical opinion is united. Ms Golightly is currently unfit for trial, and likely to remain that way. Is that as you see it?'

'Yes, Your Worship. I draw Your Worship's attention to Dr Robertson's report, page three, paragraph fifteen: Despite being medicated with a relatively high dose of anti-psychotic medication, the patient continues to insist that she must complete the cycle by killing Laura Adams – who is present in court today, Your Worship. She attempts to attack any female staff member in any way of similar appearance to Miss Adams, insisting that Miss Adams *knows too much*, and it is often necessary to sedate her. In my opinion, she is not fit to stand trial now, or in the foreseeable future.' He placed the report gently on the table before continuing. 'Your Worship, given that this is a unanimous opinion from the three eminent psychiatrists whose reports I have tendered in court this morning, I request that this case be adjourned indefinitely.'

At last, the lawyer could sit down. The defence lawyer stood up, bowed slightly and said, 'We have no objection, Your Worship.' He sat down again, and Laura wondered how much he was being paid for that little appearance, and thought maybe it would work out to about five hundred dollars a word. Maybe more.

The magistrate tapped away at his computer. Laura stopped holding her breath, as she gained confidence that she would not have to give evidence. Finally, he looked up.

'It does appear that the defendant will not be able to stand trial at this time. However, I would like to hear from the prosecution as to the pertinent facts of this case and the other allegations. If you would be so good, Mr Swayfield.'

Again, the man rose to his feet. 'As you please, Your Worship.' He opened his laptop and pressed a few buttons. From her vantage point in the court, Laura could see he had a speech already prepared.

'Your Worship, the prosecution alleges that Geranium Golightly killed Ivy Vine by hitting Ms Vine on the head with a mallet. This mallet was located, stained with Ms Vine's blood, at the scene. DNA from Miss Adams was also found on the mallet, as she was hit just prior to the arrival of the police. There is a recording from a mobile telephone in which Ms Golightly admits to poisoning Lancelot Charger by administering hemlock in tea, though it is not clear whether she intended Mr Charger to be the victim. That is a charge which might be brought later, Your Worship. In the course of the investigation, evidence was discovered which indicates that it was likely Ms Golightly also killed the mayor of her previous town by pushing him down the stairs, and may also have committed the vehicular manslaughter of her maid.'

The magistrate pursed his lips and nodded.

'Evidence suggests that Ivy Vine and Geranium Golightly came to Cowagulac for a fresh start after Ms Golightly's husband also died. Investigations are being reopened into that death, which was previously declared an accident. Your Worship, I don't wish to besmirch the name of one of the deceased, but it is apparent that Ms Vine was, if not aware, certainly suspicious, of Ms Golightly's dangerous behaviour, but chose to accompany her as a companion to Cowagulac. In hindsight, Your Worship, letting the police know of her suspicions may have preserved her life as well as that of Mr Charger.

There is just one other point I wish to make. The police involved in this case have been outstandingly vigilant in their investigations, and Constable Makepeace was a main player in ensuring that no more people died as a result of Ms Golightly's unfortunate psychiatric condition.'

He sat down and there was a smattering of applause in the well of the court, which quickly died out under the glare of the magistrate.

The magistrate looked at defence counsel. 'Do you wish to say anything?'

'No, Your Worship.' Another fifteen hundred dollars was spent.

'Very well. I declare that, at this stage, the defendant is unfit for trial, and order that these charges be deferred until, and if, she becomes capable.'

The clerk rose. 'Court is now adjourned.'

Everyone stood up as the magistrate left the court, and immediately the reporters rushed out, dialling their phones as they went. The court emptied quickly, and most of the public congregated in the nearest coffee houses to discuss proceedings.

Laura stayed in her seat. She felt empty and sad. She had enjoyed the company of the two old ladies right up till the end, and the shock she had felt when she had seen Ivy's blood-soaked body still gave her nightmares. Without being aware of it, tears began to roll down her cheeks.

Magnum was on his way out of the now empty courtroom when he saw Laura and went to sit next to her.

'You okay? It's been a tough few months.'

Unused to being given sympathy so freely, Laura found the tears falling with increasing speed and intensity, and an undignified hiccup resonated round the courtroom. Makepeace produced a plastic sachet of tissues and handed them over.

'Look, Laura, what about we go back to the station and have a cup of tea? I think the sarge might even have something stronger we could add to it.'

Laura looked up, red-eyed. 'That would be nice. Thank you.'

Epilogue

One thing led to another, and six months later, Magnum and Laura were quietly married in the Cowagulac chapel. Laura was still surprised at having acquired a husband.

They moved to Balsham. Makepeace had been promoted there after his excellent detective work in the Geranium case. 'Magnum,' Laura approached him tentatively one evening. 'There's something I wanted to tell you.'

Magnum had learned early on in his relationship with Laura that this was prelude to an announcement which he suspected he wouldn't like. 'Yes?' he said suspiciously.

'In honour of your work in our murder case, I've applied to join the police force. I need your help to lose thirty kilos, though, so I thought we might start with a brisk walk. Come on.'

She headed out the door. Magnum sighed and slowly got to his feet.

'I thought she was going to say she was pregnant,' he muttered.

Laura turned back. 'I am.'

About the Author

R osemary is a commerce teacher and school counsellor. She has taught in Canada and England, and worked as an au paire in Germany. (Her pre-employment German lessons resulted in one phrase committed to memory – "Mein auto ist kaput!")

In past iterations of her life, she has been an avid singer, director and performer. She enjoys gardening, knitting, bike riding, and of course writing and reading. Rose has travelled widely, including through Antarctica, Iceland, Greenland, Alaska and North Korea.

For several happy decades she and her husband Peter sang, travelled and taught singing, until Peter's untimely death in 2002. Although this is the first book Rose has published, she has four more in the pipeline.

Acknowledgements

To members of the Boroondara Writers Group, who patiently sat through readings of the book each month. Their suggestions often helped me make sense of the manuscript.

9 781923 501096